VOLUNTEER

About the Author

Gary McElkerney was born and raised in Belfast, Northern Ireland, where he gained a BA Hons. in Furniture, Product and Interior Design at the University of Ulster, before pursuing a career in lighting design. He considers himself a storyteller more than an author, and his experiences volunteering for first aid work in Nicaragua, Hungary, and Ethiopia gave life to 'Volunteer'.

Gary continues to live, and work as a Lead Lighting Designer, in Belfast. His hobbies include playing American Football for the Carrickfergus Knights, and taking part in endurance races around the UK and Ireland, raising funds for charity.

Volunteer's publication is the first phase of a wider project, The Ultimate Creative Challenge; to write a novel and get it published, to develop a script and produce a film or TV drama, and record songs for a soundtrack album.

You can find out more on his Facebook page **www.facebook.com/UltimateCreativeChallenge**, or follow him on Twitter **@TUCC2013**.

VOLUNTEER

By Gary McElkerney

Write Path NI Limited

VOLUNTEER

Copyright © 2013 Gary McElkerney. All rights reserved.

First paperback edition printed 2013 in the United Kingdom.

A catalogue record for this book is available from the British Library.

ISBN 9780992782405

No part of this book shall be reproduced or transmitted in any form or by any means, electronic or mechanical, including photocopying, recording, or by any information retrieval system without written permission of the publisher.

Published by Write Path NI Limited

For more copies of this book, please email:
info@writepathni.com

Cover designed by Gary McElkerney

Images by Drew Heaslip, ICON Images

Printed in Great Britain

Although every precaution has been taken in the preparation of this book, the publisher and author assume no responsibility for errors or omissions. Neither is any liability assumed for damages resulting from the use of this information contained herein.

Acknowledgements

Writing Volunteer was a cathartic and challenging experience that would not have been possible without the support of my friends. I would like to thank every one of you who helped me along this journey; those who endured my extremes from me being reclusive, to constantly bending their ear about writing, and those that gave me strength, through the frustrating times of struggle and doubt. You propped me up, pulled me through, and kept me moving forward.

I would like thank my family, particularly my parents. Thank you for your encouragement, for your wisdom and guidance. You have presented me with every opportunity to succeed in life and as people you inspire me the most. No words can convey my heartfelt thanks.

Thanks to my secret weapon, Janine Cobain whose enthusiasm and dedication to Volunteer inspired me to push ahead. Thank you for your encouragement, your belief and your invaluable assistance.

Thank you to Drew Heaslip from ICON Images for an amazing 'Volunteer inspired' photo-shoot. A fabulous experience magnified by his enthusiasm for photography and professionalism. Also, thanks to Grant Quinn and Anthony Brown for help with props and effects, although their enjoyment at smashing me in the face with cement mix, throwing stones, and trying to set me on fire was disturbing.

Thanks to all the test readers, your reviews helped to shape the novel and gave me confidence to move it in the right direction.

To Write Path NI Limited, thank you for publishing Volunteer and giving me the opportunity to get across the finish line.

For those that doubted me, thank you; negativity is often as powerful as positivity and at times a great motivation.

I hope this novel inspires you to think big, to dream big and to want to **be** more. It is not easy, it takes time but, with hard work and perseverance, and the humility to accept help when you need it, you will succeed.

Dedicated to volunteers everywhere, especially those who have lost their lives trying to make the world a better place.

"Volunteering is a worldwide concept. It is not the sole responsibility of one country or organisation, nor does it need a specialist skill set. It is everywhere, all levels of ability, experience and qualifications."

Gary McElkerney

Chapter 1: The End, The Beginning

I was at peace, that feeling between being asleep and awake. Wrapped in a duvet of calm, a gentle breeze teased my exposed skin and the sea whispered a comforting melody.

The darkness dissolved into a kaleidoscope of black and orange that danced in front of my eyes.

How long had I been sleeping?

I was at the beach, wasn't I? My consciousness stirred. When had I come to the beach?

Despite the crippling exhaustion, curiosity got the better of me; I mean, this was pretty anti-social, and a pale-skinned Northern Irish man laid cooking in the sun was a recipe for disaster. I forced open my eyes; a hazy silhouette loomed over me.

Was that Michael?

What the hell was he doing here? When did…? Where was…?

"You dumb motherfucker! You're lucky to be alive." The words echoed inside my head.

He moved, taking my shade and forced me to lift my heavy arm to block out the piercing glare of the sun. Confused, I squinted to focus. Dried blood and white powder covered my arm. Was that sulfa powder? Was it my blood?

My brain cranked into action and a surge of pain washed over me as the channels to my senses gushed open.

That sound of the sea, lapping the sand, was the roaring engine of Medical Aid Africa's 4x4, and I was sprawled in the back of the trailer, being buffeted from side to side, wincing with discomfort as we hit any uneven surface.

I had surfaced into the nightmare that was my reality; a life beyond the safe compound of my dreams and as I fought to speak, a dazed confusion enveloped me.

"What happened?" I knew it was over. Done. I'd fucked up!

Volunteer

Three Weeks Earlier

Why did these trips always start ridiculously early? Seriously, 5:00 am on a summer's morning? Stuck in the car with my parents and their barrage of questions; had I remembered my passport? My Malaria tablets? The inventory list continued, as did my half-assed answers and I responded like a recorded message. This wasn't my first time away, and they knew me well enough to know I would be organised to ensure I got a decent night's rest before the arduous trip ahead. The questions were to disguise their own nervousness, I knew that.

I closed my eyes and hoped to catch a few moments sleep, the hypnotic pulse of the orange street lights filtered through my eyelids. Mum drowned out the faint mumble of the car radio as she lectured Dad on one of his many bad habits. I concentrated hard on blocking out Mum's drone, a skill passed on from my dad. I displayed many of his traits, unconsciously moulding myself around him. Occasionally, I opened my eyes to get my bearings as we drove, first taking a guess at how far we had progressed on a route well-travelled.

We reached our destination and Dad swung the car swung into a parking space with ease. I shook myself awake ready to step into 'happy family' mode. I knew how to act the part; I just didn't feel it. I wasn't an abused child, nor were my parents' alcoholics. We weren't a family caught up in the so-called 'Troubles' or recovering from a split, nor was I a child forced to exist under a regimented routine, to be seen and not heard, with no time for fun. I was just at that age where I was done with the family phase and wanted to be left alone to 'find myself', as clichéd as that sounded.

Sleepily, I pushed the seatbelt release and rubbed my eyes. On any journey I dozed, and always woke up with my contact lenses stuck to dry eyeballs. Not a comfortable feeling, but still better than the alternative; I hated wearing my glasses, associating them with the problems I had growing up. The sentiment that 'True beauty comes from the inside' was very noble, but if you were a kid with freckles, serious acne, a comb over hair style and glasses - the stereotypical nerd who was always picked last - then it didn't really cut it.

I shook my arm free from the seatbelt, stepped out of the car and zipped up my jacket as far as it would go, pulling at the cuffs to cover my hands from the early morning chill. I lifted my bag from the boot and, despite it having wheels, I carried it. I didn't want to be associated with the over-tanned, immaculately groomed men that you saw

Volunteer

walking confidently through airports, wheeling their little handbags along behind them. The scary thing was those guys weren't even gay, just posers. A new breed of twenty-first century man, who seemed to love themselves a bit too much, attempting to adopt a gay image, without over doing the flamboyant traits.

Dad sensed it was all about the image and pushed the bag off my shoulder. I over-balanced and crashed, thunderously, into a shuttered shop front. Mum spun around on her heel and glared at us. I pointed at Dad in a childishly futile attempt to deflect her stare, and we followed her into the youth club, laughing quietly.

As we entered the hall, what struck me first was the horrendous lime green carpet - they must have been given it for free, why else would they have it? We assembled with the other volunteers and their parents and I basked in the awkwardness. It was amusing watching the rest of the group struggle with the situation. I had known them long enough to remember some of their names, most of them were a couple of years younger and it was funny to see how they conducted themselves in front of their parents.

I had signed up to the team late, as one of the leaders, due to my experience on two previous trips, but I wasn't really into this trip. I had planned to concentrate on my final year in university; I figured I would be working hard and a holiday first would be good. I had attended the odd meeting and one or two fundraising nights, but never felt part of the group. They were told that I was drafted in as team medic, with stories of bravery and heroism. They would find these stories had elements of truth, but were over-exaggerated, but I would preserve the image of a mysterious guy, brought in to save the day, for a while longer.

We were joined by Colin and Roisin, my fellow team leaders, who had pulled this group together from the community, people who had responded to the advert on a poster at college.

Colin was tall, and had recently got in to shape, which was bizarre, as a month in Ethiopia would sort out anyone's weight issues. He was a strange man, the oldest at thirty-two, his beard aged him further, yet he had an immature way of talking and connecting with the group. He even dressed as 'one of the kids', with baggy, brown combat trousers, trainers and a humorous T-shirt printed with a comical cartoon version of Evil Knievel. Single and living with his mother, Colin was a career driven individual, dedicated to working with young people and once you got to know him, his

Volunteer

passion for his work was evident, as was his reputation for truth and patience. He had a genuine appreciation of the pressures young people faced growing up.

At twenty-six, Roisin was younger than Colin and had almost compulsive organisational skills, which would ensure this trip was a success. She was tall for a girl, slim, with short-cropped hair and came across as quite shy. Her appearance helped her blend in with the rest of the group, but the large blue file she held to her chest gave her away as being in charge. Roisin was single, training to become a teacher, and the more mature of the other two leaders. But a people person she was not, and on this trip I would discover that, despite her authoritative stature, she lacked patience and understanding.

As Colin spoke I stared into space, partly tired, but mainly bored. I tuned in at the sound of my name 'Chris Johnston, Team Medic' and nodded with reverence and modesty as he introduced me to the parents, and as he continued I zoned back out to my open-eyed dream state. I hadn't picked up on what he was saying, but I was well-versed with previous trips; breaking the ice with a few jokes, thanks offered up for funds raised and of course prayer time. There was always prayer time.

Hypocritically, I bowed my head and waited for the part where I was programmed to say 'Amen' with convincing dedication.

I had never claimed to be a devout Christian, I played lip-service by going to mass every Sunday, on holy days, and during lent. You picked a side to even up the numbers, the all-important extra vote. My parents were Catholic and they were more in tune with their religion since the death of their parents, as if it was a form of communication with them.

The bus waited outside the hall, its engine hummed with anticipation, doors folded outwards onto the footpath, awaiting our luggage. I ducked under the doors and threw my case into the compartment. I impressed no-one. It wasn't a show of my strength; I was just desperate to get onto the bus. I stood beside my parents for a moment, and watched the others, as if picking up tips on how to deal with the goodbyes, but when we were called to board I played it like a natural. I bent down and gave mum a hug and a kiss on the cheek, gave dad a firm 'we don't do hugs' handshake. Mum issued warnings about my behaviour, my manners and personal safety that were answered with my usual sarcastic humour, in return I got a cutting glare from

Volunteer

her and a 'wise up' look from Dad, who smirked with amusement.

I climbed into the fully carpeted interior of our transport and watched through the tinted windows as the last few team members wrestled their bags into the underbelly of the bus. These were the ones who would struggle, especially in the first week, and the reluctant bus driver was forced to help.

I sat with the boys at the back of the bus, beside the emergency exit, partly because it has more leg room, partly so I had my escape route sorted if we crashed. A bit morbid maybe and this sense of self-preservation futile when I didn't wear a seatbelt, but then who does on a bus? With everyone loaded and the waving done, the bus crept away from the kerbside.

We were on our way.

Chapter 2: Escape From Normality

For this trip we had travelled a hundred miles, on the bus from Belfast to Dublin, to catch a flight to London Heathrow, and then on to Addis Ababa via Rome.

I bought a new book for the journey, another to add to the pile at home I had yet to finish. I wouldn't finish this one either, but it was part of the ritual. I chose a crime book; the front cover was strangely appealing, depicting bloodied finger tips sliding down a shower curtain.

The flights were routine; I'm not a great lover of flying, just the take-off. Being sucked into my seat as the pilot 'put his foot down' was the closest I was going to get to being a fighter pilot, a childhood dream that was destroyed by the curse of visionary aids. I did love the contrast as you broke through cloud cover and were welcomed by clear blue skies, and then there was the turbulence; Flax attacks. The adrenaline rush as the plane dropped without warning was exquisite; I would have put my arms up in the air and screamed with delight, but in today's post 9/11 paranoia, I risked being arrested for trying to bring the plane down with over enthusiasm.

After twenty-five hours we arrived in Ethiopia and first impressions were good. One of the cleanest and most modern airports I had been in, very spacious, although being empty might have helped and the staff treated us like movie stars, probably because there were more of them than passengers. They were all neatly dressed, well-presented and hustling for a tip. The interior was decorated with stunning oversized pictures promoting the African nations, their colours and culture. Not that I was expecting pictures of war, famine and poverty, but I wasn't really expecting this either.

We huddled around our bags and Colin called me over to introduce two men, Amare and Negasi, who were our guides and in-country representatives. Both men were very different; Amare, the younger of the two, was more confident and well-groomed in jeans and red T-shirt, taking the lead with introductions. Negasi looked like one of the working men from the promotional posters for the charity. He was tall and thin, his clothes almost worn out, wearing sandals. Yet, as quiet as he was, he was more approachable, with a respectful nature, using religious gestures as a way of greeting and showing thanks.

We left the air-conditioned airport for the stifling, humid heat of the Ethiopian sun. Some of the girls had the sleeves of their T-shirts rolled up, those with confidence had changed into vest tops - not registering the disapproving looks of the locals. For the guys, we just added sunglasses. Instantly cool.

We walked the short distance to the car park, and everyone climbed into the van to get out of the heat. I hung back and helped Amare, passing luggage up to Negasi, who stood on the roof of the bus. I watched them cover the luggage with a blue tarpaulin sheet.

"Get much rain here?" I enquired.

Amare smiled. "Protection from sun, and the locals."

———

With everyone crammed into the van, we travelled along the lengthy driveway to the main airport gate. Negasi drove, and through the tinted windows I saw a line of soldiers, dressed in blue camouflage, armed with AK47s and seated, crossed-legged around the perimeter of airport.

"That's a lot of soldiers," Mark said.

"They're more like police," I explained. "They're Federals, the government's private army." I knew that from reading up on the country; I had an annoying habit of doing research. It was annoying because I only took in the useless information; the wonders of the internet.

We travelled through the city, which was observed with a mixture of emotions and opinions on the bus. Surprised at the poverty, surprised by the wealth, surprised at the greenery, everything they thought they knew about Africa was being rewritten. I too was being re-educated, the greenery and decent roads were unexpected.

After previously spending a month in Central America, I was used to the slums and how the smell sticks with you. You could tell a lot about the economic status of a country by its building layout. From a distance, the high-rise buildings gave the city a similar appearance to any other, but it was when you got down to ground level that the poverty-stricken faces were visible, the poorly constructed buildings erected around more prominent ones, to almost emphasise their importance and architectural prowess. Then, you had the slums; a collection of structures made from scavenged materials, sticks, wire and wood, that resembled tree huts from childhood. These, unfortunately, were home for hundreds of families, and took up every available inch of space.

Eventually, we arrived at the Hotel Lalibela and apart from the standard reception area, with the desk, trolleys, signature carpet and uniformed porters, the hotel was more like a gated set of apartments. The building was new, five storeys high, and painted white to deflect the sun.

The lobby of the hotel was in perfect condition, though the outside had never been considered. There was a rough perimeter wall with cement thrown between the lazily stacked bricks. A miss match of concrete slabs served as a patio, with cheap, cupid-style plaster statues and two dark-green, plastic patio sets, the type you got from a DIY store, their colour bleached out by the sun. And of course no cheap patio set is complete without a green and white striped parasol.

Volunteer

Most of the team rushed from the cool van to the tinted glass doors of the hotel. Negasi crouched on the top of the bus and slid the bags off the roof one at a time. I took them, standing on the ladder at the back of the bus with my right arm hooked round the steps to keep me in place. I grabbed at anything to get a hold of on the bags, a strap or a loose part of a bag before letting it swing and drop into the waiting hands of the chain gang - formed by the guys and a hotel porter, who had sniffed out the potential for a tip. He wore a red jacket with a gold trim which reminded me of the Royal Irish military jackets, and a pair of the whitest trousers I had ever seen, with polished black shoes.

Inside, Amare stood with Roisin at the reception. She was flicking between pages of her blue file, occasionally lifting the thin metal bar to open the clasps and remove a page. Amare was acting as the middleman, taking the pages from Roisin and passing each one to the receptionist.

Roisin had paired up the girls and they disappeared to their rooms. She had partnered me with a gangly sort of guy named Paul, whose hair possibly weighed more than his entire body, and whose face was plastered in sun cream. At least I wasn't with Colin. I wanted to be seen as just another member of the team, which would allow me some insight into how everyone was really settling in.

I took the key from Roisin, which was attached to an oversized plaque, more like a plank of wood, with the room number written very small in red marker.

I dragged my bag, and the key, and its plank, behind me up the stairs, mentally and physically exhausted from the travelling. I wheeled my bag down the hall, marvelling at the style of the interior. It was very cheap and outdated, patched up with whatever they had salvaged.

We came to our room - the brass numbers were at least in the right place, but were nailed to what looked like a sheet of MDF. We didn't need a key; we could have knocked the door through with the plank. The room wasn't much better, two single beds covered in heavy, embossed fabric throws and curtains to match. It was clean, and at least the bathroom was modern. At the end of the day, it was a room with a bed, and somewhere to put my head down. I was never one for fancy hotels; years of team sports and lads' weekends away had acclimatised me to cheap hotels, with the attitude that once my eyes were closed and I was asleep everything would be OK.

Volunteer

I dropped my bag at the bottom of the bed closest to the window, and furthest from the door, and lay down, relieved to take the weight off my poor limbs after the journey from hell. I folded my arms behind my head and closed my eyes.

Chapter 3: Initial Warning

We had finished our breakfast of fresh fruit and dry rolls, and were looking forward to a visit to the Building 4 Hope's affiliate office, when Amare appeared, speaking with some urgency to Colin and Roisin in the lounge. A student protest had descended into violence nearby and the Federals had attacked one hundred and fifty civilians, with twenty-five of those, allegedly, shot. We made the decision to move the team a day early, to Dessie, which lay fourteen hours north of Addis Ababa.

Despite the apparent danger we remained calm and packed the bags and the team efficiently onto a pimped-out school bus painted green and white. It had a few miles under its belt all right and it had been battered along the gauntlet of life. With the luggage piled under the trusty tarpaulin and roped down to hold it all in, we set off.

Volunteer

The first hour was taken up with gossip and storytelling, comparing each other's social scars and personal achievements, selling ourselves just to be accepted on an equal level within the group. I always had stories to tell, adding a comedy slant to make them sound better than they actually were. I was a good storyteller, and people were often amazed by what I had achieved. In reality, I wouldn't wish my life on anyone.

Things quietened down and it was time for music and taking in the surroundings. I admired this new country and I longed to find some association with this place that was so different from my life at home.

After numerous toilet stops, lunch at a guarded hotel, and some close shaves with cliff edges, the day darkened. The travelling tin can had carpet and tassels, hanging decorations and pictures, but no air conditioning and the heat had taken its toll on the group. As the more comfortable evening temperatures offered the opportunity for the team to get some sleep, I was left with the silence of my thoughts.

The mind is a work of genius to have accomplished so many things. It is also our worst enemy; it has the power to install doubt, incite jealousy and diminish our mental strength. Our grip on reality weakens and rational thinking falters, our mind is equally creative and destructive.

I thought of home, not because I was missing it, I never got homesick. I'd go as far as to say I hated Northern Ireland, but didn't have the guts to pack up and leave for good. I thought of my recent break up and wondered who she was shagging now, and I thought of the girls who had preyed on my vulnerability and desperate need for attention. Like a fool, I had jumped at the comfort of intimacy, only to be a notch on their social bed post - I'm not complaining or saying that I was some kind of stud; I certainly wasn't God's gift to women, far from it. Starting a conversation with a woman was difficult enough for me, but once I was given the opportunity, I would pour out my personality to draw them in. But right now, I didn't have time for any of that, what with me being away saving the world and all.

I thought of death; my death. The type of death that was scripted in Hollywood, cut down in a hail of bullets protecting a frightened child in my arms, pushing another to safety; bombs erupting, planes crashing, buildings exploding around me and how everyone who knew me would mourn my heroic death. I imagined my coffin as it came off the

Volunteer

Troop carrier to a military salute; my parents would be consoling each other in a lighting storm of camera flashes.

This would be the extreme I needed to go to in order to get noticed in my life at the minute.

Chapter 4: Dessie

6:00 am in the town of Dessie came with Islāmic Morning Prayer as the wake-up call. As persistent as an alarm clock that you cannot switch off; if I had a gun I would have silenced that speaker, not because of religious bigotry - I was from a backwards country that knew all about that - it was simply that it was six in the morning, and I wasn't a morning person. After the first annoyance, I found something reassuring and comforting about its soft, repetitive sound, it was certainly preferable to the high-pitched beep of an alarm.

I opened an eye at the sound of Paul violently tossing about his bed. Clearly, he wasn't a morning person either. I rolled on to my side to get out of bed; an old injury inhibited me sitting straight up in the morning. Thanks to a Nicaraguan opportunist, I had a wonky right shoulder-blade after he had pulled me off the back of a 4x4, trying to steal my bag, and I landed badly on my head and shoulders. He never got my bag, which was no consolation to the pain I had endured self-healing, mind you. We were building a medical clinic out there, so the faster I worked, the quicker I would get medical care. Almost ironic.

I reached for my glasses from the old bedside cabinet and reluctantly slid them on my face and looked around. The high bedroom ceiling was painted an off white with wooden bracing for support, or decoration, on pale green walls. Sunlight streamed through a tall window beside my bed that was open, but the French lace curtains were still. The room contained two wooden framed beds, the bedside cabinet and a sink by the door. There wasn't a wardrobe though, so I would be living out of my wardrobe with wheels for the duration of the trip, my imagination convincing me that tarantulas and other insects would live in my clothes and shoes. At least it would save time on packing.

Paul had buried his face in the pillow and went back to sleep. As I came out of the bathroom I thought of kicking, or throwing something at him, but I didn't know him well enough. There was a danger of him taking it badly and kicking my ass so I took a more civilised approach.

Gary McElkerney

I grabbed his shoulder and arm and shook violently, bouncing him into the mattress.

"Paul! Fuck sake, wake up, get up!"

"What! What's wrong?" alarmed he kicked at the bed sheets, flailing about like a fish out of water.

"Time to get up, it's a beautiful morning," I calmly replied.

He flopped back into the bed, exhausted by his burst of energy.

"You're hilarious," Paul said, as he mustered a laugh and shook his head, dragging himself out of his bed.

I pulled on my weathered blue Snickers trousers, still in good condition after two trips, and a cheap Primark T-shirt. I turned my steel toe-capped desert boots upside down and tapped the bottom, making sure nothing had taken refuge inside, before I pushed my feet in them. They were scuffed, covered in cement and dirt from doing work around my parents' house. I lifted my cheap sunglasses and my ever-faithful Canadian Roots cap and threw them into my backpack with my factor 30 sun cream. As a pasty white Northern Irish guy I was,

Volunteer

on occasions of carelessness, prone to supporting a lobster red colour change, a golden tan was available only in a can to guys like me.

A make-shift medical kit, containing Medi-packs, sterile water, plasters, Imodium plus, blackcurrant Dioralyte and rubber gloves, accompanied the sun cream. Finishing off my essentials was a pair of Kuny's working gloves, the cotton gloves with the blue latex dip over the palm side of the hands for extra grip. I liked them because they didn't cause blistering like the heavy-duty rigger gloves, useful with me having 'girly sensitive hands' and all that, as my dad would joke.

Once I was ready, I turned my attention to Paul. He wore black combats, two pairs of socks, desert boots, a white T-shirt two sizes too big and a green fishing style hat. Clearly, this was Paul's first trip and I was the veteran sergeant working with a private who had never seen action. I motioned to look in his bag and as I took things out Paul protested that he needed them, as if his life depended on it.

"You'll get water on site, use your highest sun cream this week, After Sun is for the evening so leave it here. A fleece? Really? Yes, it's winter here, but this is Africa, and you're Northern Irish. Save your T-shirts and leave your camera. It'll get destroyed or stolen."

"But I want photos of what we did here," whined Paul.

"Then get a disposable camera. Trust me, by the end we'll all get each other's details and keep in touch and be best friends for life. You'll get a copy of most people's photos."

We made our way down to the dining room, a young, black woman stood at the reception desk, smiling, and her open palm directed us to a door on the right. This must have once been a large house; walls had been knocked through to open up the ground floor into a lounge, a small dining area, and a bar. Most of the team were already seated, and the girls that were here already were well-presented, with hair done and make-up carefully applied. I admired their enthusiasm, but that dedication wouldn't last long. The need to sleep in the mornings would quickly take priority.

Breakfast was two fried eggs or porridge, and although porridge with water was always wrong in my eyes, it was the more sensible choice for a decent breakfast. This was our first 'slumming it meal, and it was the time you recognised the 'silver spoon' children.

"I'm not eating that," Lisa said.

Lisa was the type that would never go camping because she needed her hair dryer and straighteners. She was tall and naturally beautiful, despite the heavy make-up. She might have the credentials of a model physically - and unfortunately mentally - but no way was she a humanitarian.

"You need to eat," I advised.

"Not in a million years will I eat that," she snapped, pushing the bowl away.

"True, you won't eat it for a few days or even for a week, but you will the week after."

It was always this way. But if she thought breakfast was bad, wait till the on-site lunches or worse the 'native' dinners. Suddenly, breakfast would become her saving grace and the all-important meal of the trip, never mind the day. I knew this first hand from my maiden trip to Central America, when a month's supply of breakfast bars had run out in the first week. My saviour was a small shop up the street from our hotel that sold cans of apple juice, Pringles and bags of soft, chewy, fruit sweets. Hopefully we would find a shop nearby to stock up on supplies.

Outside was a crisp blue sky, not a cloud in sight - a fine summer's day back home, but this was at 7:00 am. We left the guarded hotel entrance in our party bus, driving past two men, who looked like extras from an American gangster movie, in oversized clothing and armed with the weapon of choice, the AK47. I looked back at our hotel. Curled paint, patched up with pieces of masonry and in places the bare iron skeleton of the building showed. Everything about the hotel appeared to have been refurbished with borrowed parts. Once a state house for a consulate, it was given to the people of Dessie to convert into a hospital, which explained the strange layout of the rooms. Eventually, even the hospital didn't want the building and so it was sold and converted into a hotel.

This isn't the part where I tell you there was distant wailing, or that ghosts roamed the corridors at night. Well, not that I noticed during my stay.

Chapter 5: On Site

We travelled for half an hour, amazed at how busy life was in Dessie at 7:00 am. It was morning rush hour, and most of the shops were already open for business. Screaming kids, dressed in tattered clothing, greeted us, waving plants and flowers in the air. Their enthusiastic reactions weren't like the charity advertisements with their sad music, suffering kids, and the soft voice of an actor pleading for your money so they can have school uniforms. Women wailed and clapped while some of the men grinned, but others stood with stern faces and monitored the staged performance.

We watched the procession ceremonies, blessing prayers, dancing and introductions in Amharic - one of Ethiopia's eighty languages. We played the rich white man, paraded about like a new toy and waited on hand and foot. I hated standing in front of everyone and trying to sell myself to an older generation who didn't speak much English or care, and the kids were too caught up in the excitement to take anything on board. I was making excuses, in truth, I hated public speaking, and specifically, I hated my accent. Hearing the Northern Ireland accent on TV was cringe worthy enough, and worse was hearing my own accent played back to me.

I wasn't here to be made to feel good. The life changing process for me came from changing someone's life through hard work, or so I told myself. Once we got our instructions from Amare that we were to dig foundations I was away, gloves and sunglasses on, cap turned backwards and shovel in hand.

I pictured the scene like a movie reel, confident stride in slow motion, locals staring at the team in awe. Their heroes had arrived. In reality no one was looking. Everyone had their jobs to do and we were another bunch of tourists, playing a part to try and restore their faith in humanity.

The local people in these countries amazed me and would put you to shame. Okay, so they were used to the work and the weather, but still, they had a job to do and they were very efficient in doing it without rest, food or water for what seemed like months. From the other trips I had learnt a great deal in getting to grips with their techniques, keeping my mouth shut, watching intently and then replicating them.

Other teammates were not so lucky. Most spent the day leaning on a shovel, or sitting around trying to make conversations with people who didn't speak English, bar the odd recognition of global words like Liverpool or Manchester United, basically anything football related. Fired up at making a connection, the excited team member would race through all the players' names. This resulted in a conversation between the locals followed by laughter, which they joined in nervously, knowing they were taking the piss.

Their enthusiasm to learn the language was admirable, but eventually you got to grips with an unofficial sign language as your social perspective changed to more of a working attitude, trying to earn some respect from the locals. If you didn't you were left to fetch things or be used as the on-site child minder to keep the kids out-of-the-way.

Lunchtime drew in. This was no picnic in idyllic surrounds; we were given a slice of beef between two pieces of bread with an apple, or other fruit. We ate in one of the late staged buildings, a concrete shell with a corrugated roof that was used as a site store for tools and cement bags. The houses were built much like any other, but with simple materials. A foot deep trench for the entire space of the house was dug out with nine deeper holes for the foundations, eight around the perimeter and one in the centre. A frame made of stripped baby trees, lined together with thin wire holding them in place, was covered in a mud and straw mix, poking holes in to let it breathe and avoid cracking. The roof was manufactured off site then added, and stones were broken up and placed in the base of the house and covered in concrete. Finally, bars or shutters were placed over the windows and an iron door added, job done. The only thing to do after that was to paint the houses, which was left to the new home owners. It was a way for them to make it their own.

Endlessly chewing on my lunch, I watched the locals work in the midday sun. We were located out of their view, either to hide the fact we had food and water, or to keep us out of the heat. We finished up and sat in cool dark silence, getting what rest we could on the bags of cement, until we were given our afternoon instructions.

We split up, but the boys stuck together to work, without local help, digging out one of the trenches for a new house. I figured this was an opportunity for the locals to get a look at four white

Volunteer

guys struggling in the heat, to boost morale and confidence, as a source of entertainment for them. We worked on opposite corners of a trench that Negassi, a man of many talents, had lined out for us. This task gave me the opportunity to see what sort of people I was working with.

First, there was my roommate Paul, the sheltered Protestant, an only child from an upper class family. This was life changing for him, not because it was charity work in a third world country, but because he was free from the worried constraints of his parents, who sheltered and hid him from the dangers of the real world, burying him in school books. No doubt one day, he would follow in his father's footsteps as a minister, or become a doctor. He worked hard, not just to fit in, but because he wanted to be seen as an equal. While he proved himself on site, his social standing and mannerisms would keep him from fully immersing into conversations, with the fear that his inexperience on certain subjects would show and embarrass him.

Mark was your typical farmer type; big leather hands, and no stranger to manual labour. He was bigger than all of us in muscle mass, and prep talked himself with every shovel of dirt he flung to the side. A friendly guy, and Christian by birth right only, he had as much interest in religion as I did. He worked happily in his bright yellow and white Antrim GAA football top showing the tanned, farmer arms to go with it. He wore a pair of black and dark grey camouflaged shorts with pasty white tree trucks for legs. He was happy to be away from home and establishing there was more to life beyond his local village, but never faltering in the belief that his farm was the centre of the world.

Finally, there was Ross, who had already given up digging. He was the talkative one, carrying much of the conversation, and was genuinely a nice guy, but not someone I had much time for. He was about my height, but a little stockier. Long dirty fair hair, just shorter than shoulder length, he was the stereotypical dope smoking type and with the rugged beard to go with it. Dressed in his bright red charity T-shirt, he had got for free at a fundraising event and a pair of baggy khaki military shorts. He was a guy with no drive or ambition, constantly blaming events in his life for his current problems.

This time he had 'pulled' a muscle in his shoulder and aggravated an old sporting injury, which would be plausible only he wasn't the sporty type - he was one of those guys who deliberately forgot their PE kit to avoid sports. Ross was a guy that did his research, any interest anyone mentioned he would claim as his own, a lifelong fan. It was a

Volunteer

desperate attempt to fit in, but also a form of manipulation, with the long list of fictitious sob stories to reach out to the easily led. There was a use for a guy like this on site, our personal errand and water boy.

The day usually finished at 4:00 pm with a game of football with the kids or hair braiding, for those who knew how, for an hour, but I worked as close to 5:00 pm as possible. I liked kids; I had a three-year old nephew whom I adored, he was the funniest little person I had ever met and his personality developed daily. I don't know why, but I had no personal interest in these kids, or their families. I was here to do a job, and I put my time in. My nature was not to mix work with fun. There was plenty of time after work to play with the kids, or maybe I was looking too objectively at it. I had a limited amount of time here and wanted to do as much as I could for these people. A little heartless, perhaps, but I didn't need to build up friendships with empty promises that weren't going to last beyond the site.

I joined in at times just to feed my competitive nature; football in forty degree heat, wearing work trousers and boots, was the perfect torment.

I already had myself an admirer though, a small boy about six years of age with a constant runny nose, who had adopted my T-shirt as his personal tissue. He wore a dirty grey jumper, with red and blue strips down the sleeves, and blue track bottoms with his ass hanging out of them. I christened him 'Snadders'.

Chapter 6: Start of Routine

We arrived back at the hotel, and I sat on the steps undoing the laces of my boots. I wasn't in any rush and sat with my arms folded across my knees, waiting for the stampede of women, trying to pull off their boots and race for the showers, to pass.

Eventually, I made my way up to the room, boots in hand, and threw them into the bathroom. We had two hours to get showered, dressed and rested before dinner; plenty of time. Then, disaster! The complaint passed from room to room that there was no hot water. I decided to improvise, and lathered up with my Christmas gift stock of Lynx shower gel, filled up a bucket with cold water and, covering up the crown jewels, I called to Paul.

"Right go for it!" I braced myself.

"Seriously, I do not want to see your penis," Paul said.

"Just get in here and throw the water over me!" I yelled.

Paul did as he was told to do, wincing with eyes half closed, he came through the bathroom door unsure of what to expect. He picked up the orange bucket and threw the contents over me. The cold water hit and I yelped, lifting my hands to wipe my eyes.

"Uh man! I saw your cock!" Paul said.

He dropped the bucket and left in disgust.

"I know you're impressed!" I called after him.

"Fuck off!" he responded, as he marched out.

Dinner was a traditional Ethiopian meal. A hot metal plate sat on, what can only be described as, an upside down sombrero, which acted as a table and we lounged around it on large floor cushions. Our stomachs rumbled as the waiters appeared with large round bowls and the contents destroyed any imaginings of a mouth-watering meal, and silenced our stomachs. It was a chicken and lamb dish, with whole eggs and other things that I guessed were vegetables, in a herb sauce on vinegar bread that had taken four days to make. It resembled the contents

Volunteer

of a baby's nappy poured on to old green underlay, khaki in colour with matching rolls, like little hot towels on an aeroplane, to lift up the food.

The meal did not go down well with the team and many of them left the dining room, showing what a rude and ignorant race us westerners could be - we had come to this country to immerse ourselves in their culture and we snubbed food that had taken our hosts four days to prepare. I wasn't a fan of this meal, but I made a dent in it. I stole everyone's unwanted vinegar bread, and washed it down with ridiculous amounts of Fanta. I made an effort, at least and out here, you needed to eat.

We finished off the night with 'reflection', a Christian led session of thanksgiving and prayer. The meeting was carried out so that it suited both denominations within the group, but tied in more with the thoughts and emotions of the team, and each of us prepared something personal to share with the others. I had never taken much interest in religion; cynically, I viewed it as a smart way of manipulating people to give away their savings in the hope that they would pay to be saved, convinced there actually was something there when we died.

It was calming listening to someone else's prayer, as they shared their hopes and fears. Normally, I would be quick to mock it, but it genuinely amazed me how someone bestowed such strong conviction in something that I too had been brought up to believe. It was easy to spot those with strong faith, compared to the part-time Christians on the team, the ones who only prayed to God when we wanted something materialistic, or when we needed to be saved from a situation we had created.

Those meetings helped us to relax, and they prepared us, mentally, for the labouring days ahead. They allowed us to unify our fears and doubts, and supported those who struggled.

Chapter 7: Fun and Games

The toil continued, and after three days on site I found myself in the bottom corner with Ross, digging out what would become a cesspit for a communal toilet. When I say we were digging - I was digging, and Ross was keeping a watchful eye over me, chatting away as usual. He directed my attention to a commotion behind us; I climbed out of the hole and there, on site, were two black bulls. The huge creatures were fighting, going head to head, like a scene from a Spanish postcard. The local children cheered them on, and the weaker bull, knowing the fight was lost, began its retreat, towards the site.

Towards us.

I knew the myth that when a bull sees red, it's kill time, and on that day I had chosen to wear my bright red T-shirt. I had also heard that bulls were colour blind, but was I about to test the theory?

Gary McElkerney

Not a fucking chance! The locals and the team screamed at me and laughed as I set off and ran through the main site street, keeping close to the houses, and along the concrete porches, my arms swinging for power, I leapt over every gap between the houses.

I was right. The bull was after me. The cowardly bastard followed my path and was far too close for comfort. The energy gained from fear is incredibly powerful; boots - What boots? I ran as if barefooted; Forty degree heat - what heat?

Fight or flight; fight or flight?

I chose flight - head first through an open window.

Fuck that hurt!

A number of intrigued eyes watched in silence, and smiled politely as I got to my feet and dusted myself down. I tip-toed towards the door and held up my hands in apology, as I left the house, cautiously looking out for the bull. The team's rapturous laughter magnified my embarrassment.

Just another day in the life of Chris Johnston.

Volunteer

Important lessons are learnt in life either by mistake, or through experience, and on each trip two things happened. Firstly, I ended up despising a food group, such as rice in Nicaragua after eating it three times a day for a month. Secondly, I added a valuable lesson to my list of 'do's and don'ts'. On this trip the lesson learnt was 'do not get your hair cut in a foreign country'.

I visited a house that had a room with a wall that was covered in mirrors, instead of paint. One of the two tall, well-groomed men there greeted me, and offered me a seat in his computer chair as he uttered the words, "Snip, snip."

I sat down and nodded. I had no way of communicating what I wanted, but it couldn't be that hard though right?

"Trim?" I said. He picked up the electric razor. "No! Trim," I repeated, and mimed a scissor action with my fingers.

"Ah! OK," he said. He cut my hair, and when almost finished he lifted the electric razor, and used it on the back of my head. Not the edges, the back.

"Ok!" he said. A pat on the back signalled that I was done.

"How much?" I pulled a few small notes from my pocket to hint at payment.

"Ah, no my friend." He waved off the payment, pushing my hand away. Again, I offered some notes, but he refused them.

Back at the hotel, some of the team were watching television and I nodded a greeting as I headed for the stairs. Roisin called me back.

"What happened to your head?" she asked, covering her mouth as she spoke.

The group struggled to hold back their laughter.

"I got a haircut." I answered.

"Did you pay for it?" Colin asked. His voice quivered.

"No it was fr- What the fuck's wrong with my hair?" I yelled.

"You have something cut into your hair," Amare explained. He tried to keep a straight face as everyone else erupted in laughter

"I have to take a picture!" Roisin exclaimed.

Volunteer

"You can fuck off. What is it?" I asked Amare, praying there wasn't a penis shape shaved into my head.

"It says ..." Amare hesitated, "It says your name." He struggled to contain himself.

"My name?" I asked, "He didn't ask my name. Amare, What does it say?" I laughed, embarrassed.

"It's something like white boy," Amare said, "it's slang, I don't know how to translate."

"Right let's go," I said to Amare, "I need you to help me fix this."

"Trimmmmm," the barber mimicked, when we returned to the house. I grinned and shook my head, in total admiration at the prank. I ended up resembling a Jarhead after all.

The bull chase and my unfortunate visit to the barbers had created unity in the group, a common memory that would be recounted differently by each team member. It also gave Colin a chance to be the dominant male, by taking the piss out of me as he liked to be the centre of attention, especially with the women. There were moments that would put me in the limelight, but I never wanted to stay there. The team found me more approachable and he didn't like that either and so Colin had directed his ego boosting attempts at me, and at Mark, and we plotted our revenge.

As a creature of routine, Colin made it very easy for us, he held meetings at the same time each day and left his bedroom door unlocked. We took our opportunities when we could, and as Ross kept a look out, we rushed into his room, like police on a raid, frantically searching for his precious Liverpool kit and trying not to disturb the contents too much avoid suspicion. I searched his bag and around his bed, Mark searched the bathroom and Paul searched his wardrobe and drawers.

"Come on!" Ross called through the door anxiously.

"He'll be away for at least another half an hour," I said, "calm yourself down."

"You don't know that," Ross said, and pulled us out one at a time. "They might finish early, or someone might see us."

"We're definitely going to get caught with you standing in here instead of keeping dick," I said. I took this very seriously, as funny as it was; I had a point to prove.

Volunteer

"Right, what did we get?" I asked. I showed off my loot to the guys, "I got his football top and a pair of shorts."

"I got this," Mark said, holding up a towel.

"I got a jacket and a cap," said Paul and held them proudly, happy that he had been included, and was one of the guys.

"Right! To the bus!" I shouted and pointed out of the door.

We raced along the hall, down the stairs and out of the front door. We ran blindly, passed everyone, answering no one to the team bus, which was parked at the front of the hotel, in full view from Colin's window. I climbed up on to the bus' roof, and laid the football top out flat. Mark threw up the towel, and I laid it beside the jersey, and placed the hat above the top. I scrambled down the ladder, the security guard grinned at us in amusement as we saluted him, and ran back inside the hotel. Colin recovered his belongings and nothing was said about the incident, which basically defeated the purpose, so we agreed to continue, until we provoked a reaction.

Gary McElkerney

We took inspiration from the 'old school book of pranks', which included cling-film over the toilet - not very exciting, yet effective.

"Ha. Fucking! Ha!" Colin shouted at 6:00 am the next morning. "You're treading on thin ice Laurel and Hardy!"

Paul and I were confused by this wake-up call at first, as it was yelled through our bedroom wall, but as we made eye contact, we realised what was going on and laughed in triumph.

"Keep laughing!" Colin said. He saw the humour in it, but I'm sure he did not appreciate the clean-up.

We implemented our final prank flawlessly, and I was so very proud of it. We were late returning from site, and Colin skipped his shower and met with Roisin for their daily meeting in the sun room. I had meticulously formulated the plan of attack in my head. Paul accompanied me into Colin's room, while Mark kept watch. I rushed into the bathroom with an intrigued Paul behind me, he didn't need to be there, but I involved him anyway, to either take some of the blame, or to give him some of the glory when it came to telling of our heroics. I reached into the shower and lifted out

Volunteer

Colin's white shower gel, perfect for the switch. I took a small plastic bottle from my pocket, and unscrewing the lid from the shower gel I decanted the coconut scented contents into the empty bottle. No sense in wasting it.

"See if you can find his sun cream," I instructed Paul, as I concentrated on getting the thick, white line of gel into the bottle, without touching the sides, and it rippled in layers. Paul rifled around the bathroom.

"Check and see if his bag is in the room," I said, "He might have sun cream in there. If not, grab some of ours."

"I could only see his After Sun," Paul whispered, "so I went and grabbed mine."

"That will do," I said and filled his shower gel bottle with the sun cream, and replaced the lid. I returned the shower gel to where I had found it, and handed Paul the empty sun cream bottle and plastic water bottle.

"Here, pour as much of that in there as you can and then let's get out of here." Paul did as I asked, concentration and a smirk etched on his face. He played his part well.

We sat in our room and waited, each of us afraid to speak in case we missed something. We heard footsteps and Colin's voice as he shouted down the hall. This was it. We sat in complete silence, nervously picking up on every noise he made. I tried to visualise his movements within the bedroom. The shower went on. We twitched with anticipation, leaning towards the dividing wall, we waited for the reaction.

"He's in the shower," Paul said. His voice quivered with excitement. We moved closer to the wall, our ears strained.

"Bastards!" Colin screamed through the wall.

We exploded from the room in full sprint and bundled down the corridor, doubled over with painful laughter, down the stairs towards the lobby. Colin emerged wrapped in his Liverpool towel with a head full of sun cream.

"Oh you can run," he shouted down to us, "but where are you going to go? We'll be discussing this later!"

And we did, in front of the team at group therapy, to everyone's amusement.

Chapter 8: Mutiny?

By the end of the week, moods had changed, opinions were voiced, and backs stabbed. Hunger had set in. People were fed up being hot and sweaty all the time and constantly feeling dirty. You got showered and dressed in clean clothes and you were sweating again.

Some found it hard emotionally with homesickness being a factor, which I never understood. I was happy to get away from home and its problems for a while. We were going home soon enough and we would wish we were still in Ethiopia.

The challenging environment took its toll on the team members, leading to illness - real and feigned. Orlaith, a pretty blonde girl with a beautiful face, claimed she was ill, but I suspected a mixture of homesickness and missing her baby boy. I had always thought it strange that she would come on a trip like this and leave her two year old son behind. Ross was sick with something he 'couldn't quite put his finger on'. Claire, Aisling and Catherine K had period pains, but continued to work, struggling with tiredness and emotional exhaustion. Cat D, a petite, dark-haired girl, very quiet and only spoke when she could add value to a conversation, had a sore ankle. She never complained, but spent a lot of time sitting out in the open with the rest of the team on site. It was hard to force her to sit in the shade, as we were cutting her off from the group; it was bad enough during the playful lunch times, seeing her disappointment at not being able to join in the activities.

Lastly, there was Elaine, a round, bubbly, ginger-haired girl, who was extremely lively. She wasn't the best looking girl in the world, but she had the most attractive personality in the group. Matched with her Christian attitude and values, she was patient, caring, and always willing to help. She had fainted on site from severe dehydration, and to see her in such a bad way was an indicator that the team was not in good shape, and everyone was trying to cope with some degree of diarrhoea, including Colin and Roisin.

I went to Roisin's room, where she was talking to Colin.

Volunteer

"Hey Chris, what's wrong?" Colin asked, concern was written on my face.

"I think we should take the day off tomorrow," I said. "We've been all go from the moment we landed, it would be good for the team to recharge the batteries."

"We have a schedule to keep to - you know that! We can rest on Sunday, it's only a day away for God's sake," Roisin snapped.

"If people get worse with another hot day on site we can write Sunday off. I'm not sure we'd make it to site on Monday either at this rate. If we take the two days now, it will give us a chance to recharge for the week ahead. Plus, right now we all need to be near decent toilets." I directed the comment at Colin, who had disappeared regularly on site with a toilet roll in his hand.

"You may be the on-site medic, but we have a schedule to keep to. Roisin and I will make the decision on this. So, if you can run along and ask the team to get ready for going to the site tomorrow, instead of inciting mutiny, that would be great," Colin smirked at Roisin.

I was never one to roll over, and it was clear Colin had made this comment out of condescending spite and jealousy. Team members came to me with their problems or to chat about personal things, I was the medic and that came with a level of confidence, but I had that type of face - the guy with the shoulder to cry on. Instead, I was being made to feel like the messenger.

"Hold on a minute, are you forgetting I'm a leader with this team, too? I did my training as well as you, so I should be involved in a decision such as this." There were moments in my life when I took a deep breath, composed myself, and structured what I needed to say to get my point across. This was not one of those times. "As for mutiny, yeah the team have come to me, I'm more approachable. I take the time to listen to them and deal with any issues they may have. You two have been so caught up in your self-importance, acting the white man with the affiliates that you haven't noticed this team is falling apart. Mutiny? I'm the one that's got the team this far."

"You need to calm down and put things into perspective. We formed this team not you," Colin nodded at Roisin for confirmation. "With a large team we needed another leader on paper, and with your previous experience, and first aid training we killed two birds with one stone. We were quite capable of making decisions without you before we

Volunteer

got here. So, at the end of the day, you are just another working team member. Now, go and get the team out of the bar and to their beds." Colin delved into his bag as a way of dismissing me.

"Do it yourself."

I glared at Roisin as I left the room. I was furious.

I marched across the courtyard anger building with each step, fists clenched and jaw locked. I wanted to stand and scream out the fury, to punch something, or someone and ran with the thought of punching Colin in his smirking face.

I joined the rest of the team in the bar and ordered beer, as a 'Fuck you and your curfew', and sat quietly, just out of the circle of a few of the team. I picked at the label on my bottle listening to the concerns of the group, who weren't threatened by my presence. My fidgeting caught Fiona's attention,

"Everything OK?" she inquired. Heads turned to me. I focused on maintaining eye contact. Fiona had a perfect cleavage. No matter what top she wore, or how she presented herself, it was hypnotic. Mark had an annoying habit of pointing her out whenever she bent down or stretched to the point she was almost falling out of her top, and every time I looked she caught me staring. I nodded, with eyebrows raised, that everything was fine, unable to speak, my jaw fused with anger. Colin appeared and the conversational volume decreased.

"Right folks, early start tomorrow." He clapped his hands together, his mouth in an awkward smile that didn't reach his eyes. The team gathered themselves and headed to bed. He avoided my glare and instead engaged in a discussion with Paula as he climbed the stairs to the bedrooms.

Chapter 9: Introductions

I sat in the lounge to watch the 32" television, BBC News24 gave constant updates from around the world and a continuous run through of the day's events. I wasn't really watching it. I was furious; I had been used, betrayed, brought here under false pretences.

I had done the leadership training, a weekend retreat, acted the Christian and got involved in their stupid role-plays and prayer sessions, and for what? I had told everyone that I was a leader of a team going to Ethiopia. The truth as I knew it, but, obviously, not the whole truth. How would I spin this to save face when I got home? Okay, so I didn't want to be a leader, or have to deal with certain responsibilities, but I was a leader on paper.

When we had trouble in Addis Ababa I had suggested moving the group out of the city, the team came to me when they had problems or wanted a chat. Well, I would take a step back, if there were problems - I would pass them on to the true leaders of this escapade.

I was so absorbed in my own head rant that I hadn't noticed someone was talking to me.

"Mind if we join you?" An English accent, one I was not able to place. It wasn't Cockney or Scouse and those were the limit of my experience with accent geography. Three men stood before me, fitting the typical mercenary look, unwashed and unshaven. I silently cursed them for wanting to share my table,

"No, go ahead," I gestured for them to sit.

"It's strange to see a young man like you, sitting alone in this part of the country. Brian Scott."

He was the tallest of the men and reminded me of Ralph Fiennes - a handsome, well-spoken Englishman. He put out his hand and sluggishly, I stretched out and shook it.

"And this is Rob Lees and Daniel Girma."

I nodded to the other two men.

"Christopher Johnston," I said.

Volunteer

"You're Irish?" Brian was intrigued. The other two were preoccupied, drinking bottles of Castel and watching the news.

"Yeah, I'm from Belfast. Building houses for a leprosy colony with a group of students from Northern Ireland." I kept my eye on the television, pretending to watch it, hoping he would do the same.

"We're journalists," Brian said, "working on a piece about the medical agencies here and the work they do. Well, more on the conditions they are expected to work in and what, if any, help they get."

I nodded my head in acknowledgment, but had nothing to add.

"Are you involved with one of the top agencies?" he asked.

"No comment," I smirked, and we all laughed. "I have first aid training, but I'm not exactly using it to its potential. I'm here in case of emergencies."

"We're headed north to a medical clinic, they treat victims of the war, leprosy and AIDs there. We're doing a piece on MAA, sorry," he translated when he saw my look of confusion,

59

"Medical Aid Africa, they could use a guy like you. Come up with us and put those skills to better use."

Ideas flooded my head. A journalist could do a write-up on me; I would be immortalised by iconic photographs, 'Chris Johnston – Humanitarian' on the front page of a magazine. I revelled in the idea of the popularity that would follow, the talk and admiration when I got back to University. How amazing would that be on my CV? How proud would my parents be of me a national hero? This was my chance, my window of opportunity.

"You know what, that sounds good," I said. "Yeah, fuck it - I'd love to help out, thanks." Inside I jumped around like an excited toddler.

"Great. We're leaving early, 5:00 am. Meet you at reception?" 5:00 am. Typical. Brian extended his hand to seal the deal and I grabbed at it this time with enthusiasm. I had just joined their team.

"Well, I'd best get some sleep. Be a long one tomorrow," I pushed myself out of the seat and gave a cool nod to the guys as I fought to contain my excitement and casually jogged up the stairs.

Volunteer

I took the coward's way out, and left a note on Paul's bag to give to Colin and Roisin in the morning. It wasn't like I was running off on holiday; this was what I had dreamed of. I was going to make a real difference, this was my calling; destiny had brought me to Ethiopia to meet these men, to take me where the real help was needed. I packed a few clothes and toiletries into my backpack, with my camera to record proof of my heroics, and my malaria tablets. Leaving the rest of my belongings behind, I made my way to reception to meet the guys.

"All sorted?" Brian asked. I nodded. My imagination had run wild in the night and I was far from rested. We headed to the car park and climbed in the beaten up Land Rover. To this day I don't know whether it was pride, the constant search for something more meaningful to add to my pathetic life, or just an alcohol fuelled 'Fuck You!' to Colin and Roisin, but the result was the same. I made the selfish decision to leave my team; a decision I would come to regret over the course of this adventure, and to this day still do.

Chapter 10: Culture Shock

No sooner were we on the road than I was asleep, not the most sociable thing to do; it was my curse, as I seen it. Whenever I had a long journey and the car was warm, I would get comfortable and that was me out for the count. It was a 5:00 am start after all, and it was warm, so in a way it was inevitable. Everyone fell asleep for some part of our nine-hour journey, bar Daniel - the driver, so I didn't feel too bad. When I woke, Rob was still asleep. I tried to stretch without invading his space in the back seat, but more so I could lean between the front seats and check the time. It was just after 11:00 am.

I gathered myself and rummaged in my bag for a cereal bar, but I didn't have enough to offer the other guys so I just kept fumbling, pretending I was looking for something else.

Volunteer

"You forget something?" Brian asked from the front seat without turning round. I pulled out my contacts case and saline solution.

"No I'm grand, got it." I had fallen asleep with my contacts in and they were dry and uncomfortable.

Once I had regained my sight, I saw lines and lines of people all shapes, sizes, and ages sitting at the side of the road. Families, couples, groups; it wasn't a queue as there was no order or direction. They were just sitting along the line of the road in huddled groups.

"What are they waiting for?" I asked. "It's the longest bus queue I've ever seen."

"They're waiting for help," Daniel answered.

"Help with what?" I took more of an interest, trying to hide my embarrassment at the seriousness of Daniel's tone. It was the first time I had heard him speak and his strong English accent surprised me, as I had presumed he was an Ethiopian. Good old racist assumption.

"The Government promised to help them. Their farms are failing, there are no jobs so people pack up and start to leave. Well, those who can.

Then medical facilities shut down, as do the schools. These people have had enough. To stay would be the death of them."

"When is help coming? I mean what sort of help will they get?" There was an awkward pause, but I was sure he had heard me.

"It's not," Daniel said, "There isn't the money to help."

It was the first time since I had been here that I had seen poverty and desperation on such a scale. What had I signed up for? Was this the way of things to come and would I be able to cope with it? We continued, past bodies strewn at the side of the road covered in blankets, I wanted to ask the question but common sense prevailed. These people in the naturally formed gutter were dead, the living were queuing up to die.

I changed the subject and asked the guys about their background, alarming as that sounded as I knew nothing about them, yet had jumped into a jeep with them in a foreign country, going to God knows where. What if they weren't journalists, what if they were drug traffickers, fuck – human traffickers, arms dealers, or even diamond

Volunteer

smugglers? Did I want to know? What if by asking I'd be part of this?

I ran scenarios through my head and weighed up my options. I didn't have any, nor did I have any evidence to support the notions my overactive imagination was running wild with.

"So, you guys mentioned you were journalists working on a story. What do you do? Where are you from?" I blurted out.

"Well, we lied. We're not journalists," Brian answered coolly. "We are contracted by the Ethiopian government to take out opposing political targets. Our medic was killed last week and you fitted the profile perfectly."

Oh holy fuck! My insides rolled

'Jump out of the fucking car now!' my mind screamed. 'Duck and roll! Duck and fucking roll!' But my body was frozen.

I jumped at the sound of riotous laughter from the front of the car.

"Did you see his fucking face man? Properly shit himself," Daniel screeched, slapping the steering wheel. "Fucking brilliant!"

Rob woke up and rubbed his eyes. "The contract killers gag?" he asked.

"Yes," squeaked Brian, his head buried in his hands, laughing so hard he sounded like he was crying. I was partly embarrassed that I had fallen for it hook, line and sinker but, mostly thankful that they had been joking.

"Bastards!" I shook my head. "I shit my bags!" I sighed with relief through my smile. Brian had managed to gather himself stuttering into laughter as he tried to speak, wiping the tears from his eyes.

"I'm from Chester, close to Liverpool" I found this strange as I couldn't pick up a Scouse accent. "Near to the Welsh border. I'm the writer, although I'm not here to write the piece now, just to gather notes and set up interviews to get both sides of the story. Once we get back to London I'll write it up."

"So, who do you write for?"

"We've been commissioned by a medical journal to do a kind of alternative view at life beyond the medical professions in our hospitals. I think it's a PR scheme to give the first world some perspective on how good their healthcare is."

Volunteer

"I'm living in Bradford, from Manchester originally," Rob said, "and I'm the photographer, here to visually document the trip. Not incredibly exciting unless you want the technical knowledge of how to take the perfect shot?"

"Trust me, you don't," interrupted Brian. Secretly I did; I had an interest in photography and was fascinated with 'having the eye' for getting those iconic pictures.

"What about you, Daniel?"

"I'm just the taxi driver from Dessie, mate."

Brian spoke between the head rest and the door. "He's a researcher from London."

"Yes, I'm a researcher from London, I plan the trips. Where to go, who to talk to, and when we get back, I make sure the information we are printing is accurate. That's me in a nutshell. It's boring, but it pays the bills and I get regular trips away."

"And what about you, what do you do?" Rob shuffled through his bag.

"Well, my name is Chris, and I'm an alcoholic," I smirked. "I just completed my second year in uni doing graphic design - well, actually my third year in university, but second year of my course," I was getting edgy. I could talk to anyone about most things, but when it came to talking about me I got nervous and rambled, fidgeting, and constantly breaking eye contact. "And I live in Belfast with my parents."

"So, what are you doing here?"

"Building houses for a leprosy colony, team medic. Been here just under a week."

"First time?" This wasn't a conversation, Brian was conducting an interview.

"In Ethiopia, yes, well, in Africa for that matter. I've done aid work in Jinotega, Nicaragua and Dunavarsany in Hungary building houses, medical clinics, etcetera."

"You enjoy it?"

"Yeah, it's very rewarding. Makes you appreciate what you have and take for granted. I like the manual labour side of it too, plus at the end of the day, it's a free trip and an opportunity to see a bit of the world." Had I interviewed successfully? I wasn't convinced. "This is off the record right?"

Chapter 11: Helping Hand

Eventually, we arrived at a place just beyond a town called Endasilaise. I had no idea where I was, but that was the last place-name I had read off a road sign about half an hour earlier, noted in case I got lost. We pulled into the courtyard outside a white building that had patterned bricks for windows. At first I thought it was a school, like the ones I had visited in Nicaragua, but this was the medical clinic.

The place was deserted; too quiet and it raised my suspicions. Getting out of the jeep with my backpack, I took a three sixty look around, waiting for an ambush, or the realisation that everyone was dead and this was a scene from a zombie apocalypse movie. Seriously, my imagination was a curse.

It was good to get out and stretch. At the side of the medical clinic there was a line of 4x4 pick-up trucks that cried out to be washed, each with the blue 'MAA' lettering on the doors.

"End of the road for you I'm afraid," Brian announced, and motioned for me to follow him. "Come on, we'll get you introduced."

I walked around the jeep, Daniel stepped forward, putting a lit cigarette in his mouth and offered his hand. I shook it, and he removed the cigarette from is his mouth again and exhaled.

"All the best young man, stay out of trouble, if you can avoid it. Look after yourself."

"Thanks." I reached over Daniel to shake hands with Rob.

"All the best, good luck to you," he said with sincerity. I adjusted my bag, nodded and jogged to catch up with Brian.

We went into the building, through a set of double doors and a young, white woman, in full headscarf, approached us smiling. Brian tried to speak to her in Amharic, using English for words he didn't know, but as it turned out, she spoke English. He asked to see Dr Emmanuel Ferrere, and she gestured for us to wait and we stood in awkward silence. It was like being in church, afraid to speak

Volunteer

and disturb the silence; I wasn't frightened of God, but I was afraid of getting a clip round the ear from my mum.

The young lady came back and called us up the corridor, inviting us to follow her as the doctor would see us in his office. This was nothing like the movies portrayed African hospitals. No moaning bodies in the corridors, no blood or spine tingling screams, no children crying over dead relatives. The floors were tiled, with blue painted walls, white tubular metal frame beds that were dressed with white sheets and thin blue cotton blankets. Very little medical equipment on display, but everything appeared clean and peaceful. It was silent, bar the odd cough or faint footstep.

We came to a small office with an open door and a tall, well-built man, in his late forties, mid-fifties maybe, greeted us. What struck me most about him was the contrast between his white hair and sun-tanned skin.

I scanned the office, which was decorated for comfort. A well-worn sofa along one of the walls made me think this office was his accommodation as well as his working environment, and a lot of his time was spent in this office. He had a very ornate, dark wooden desk with a black leather office chair on wheels, again well worn. On the back wall above a filing cabinet there was a picture of his family, wife, son and daughter and a picture of another woman, maybe a sister.

"And this is Christopher? Chris?" He urged for a preference.

"Chris is fine."

"He's volunteered to help out," ushering me forward to shake hands with Emmanuel. He spoke perfect English, but had that French twang in his voice which was stronger over certain words.

"Have you any certificates? A résumé?"

"I don't. I have training in general first aid, practical first aid, and emergency life support if that helps." I willed him to take me on, confident in my abilities, although I had never practiced ten percent of what I had been taught, but I was well rehearsed in administering plasters and bandages.

"Well, I won't be using you in surgery, but I'm sure you could assist the nursing staff. If you take this note to Odette she'll get a room sorted and get you familiarised." He lifted a silver pen out of his trouser pocket and scribbled in circles to get the ink flowing. He wrote some instructions for Odette,

Volunteer

and then carefully ripped the note away from the scribbles, folded it in half and handed it to me with further instructions.

"Your duties will also include cleaning - we all pitch in with this. A lot of dirt blows through this hospital and it clings to everything." This explained the cleanliness of the place.

"Odette should be where you came in, if you need anything just ask and she will be able to sort you out. I'll catch up with you later."

Brian extended his hand "If I don't see you again, best of luck. We'll be travelling along the border so I might see you out on the field."

I never did though.

I made my way back down the hall, peering through doors to get a feel for the space, before arriving at the front desk. Odette wasn't there. I hated these situations, what do you do? Go looking for her and take the risk of getting lost? Go back to the office, or just wait? I wasn't going to just walk round the hospital, knowing my luck, I would end up in the psych ward, and with my mental state I'd never get out. I would appear stupid going back to the doctor's office so I decided to just stay where I was.

"Yes?" I heard a voice from behind me, thick with an unfamiliar accent - French, but distorted by a stronger, maybe English accent, alternating between words. Odette was adjusting the head scarf that she had taken off while outside. She was stunning. Not made up, but naturally beautiful; dark hair and eyes with a slim figure, a combination that always won me over. The head scarf hadn't done much for her before, but then I hadn't really been paying attention. She was more of a nurse than a receptionist, although she wasn't dressed like your typical nurse, but then again what was typical out here? The head scarf gave her the nursing image, but the rest of her clothes didn't reflect that, she wore a plain blue T-shirt with the sleeves rolled up to the shoulder and a pair of khaki three-quarter length pants. They were the same as the girls from the team had worn at nights, slim-fitting with the military look, but the pockets were just for show; too small to be practical.

"Can I help you with something?" I had stood this whole time staring at her like a creep. I handed her the note in a panic and with a quick look at it she beckoned me. "Come with me." She walked down the corridor towards the office, turning this time up a flight of stairs and along a balcony that

Volunteer

had decorative cement blocks to let in the light and air.

As we walked, I tried to think of something to say to break the ice. Normally, I would be hard to silence, but maybe it was the unfamiliar territory. I knew nothing of this place, or this girl and feared I would ask a stupid question. Or maybe it was simply because she was really beautiful and I didn't want to start off like an idiot. I was comfortable talking to women, most of my friends were female, and they saw me as the older brother, or the funny guy. But when it came to women that I found attractive, I was hopeless. Stuttering over words or struggling to string a full sentence together, or worse, saying something that had no conversational quality or any relevance, or bringing on the dreaded awkward silence.

My room at the far end of a corridor was more like a cleaning store, with no windows and a bed that must have been built in the room because there was no other way to get it in there, and a small bedside cabinet with a locking compartment. Pointless when you could lift the whole cabinet and run with it, or rip the MDF back off it and steal whatever was inside.

"Is there anything else I can get you?"

How about a different room?

"No, no I have everything I need. Thanks. Anything I can help you with?"

"No, but I'm sure a nurse will be along soon for you to assist."

"Cool, sounds good. Thanks," I nodded.

"Okay then." With that she spun on her heel and headed down the corridor.

As I listened to her fading footsteps I buried my head in my hands. 'Anything I can help you with?' There was that stupid question crap. 'Anything I can...' What Chris? What could she possibly need help with? Walking back to the reception area in case she got lost? Holding the air she needed to breathe? She wasn't carrying anything else for you to give her a hand with. Fucking idiot! I wished, not for the first time that for once my brain would actually work in a situation like that, allowing me to appear cool or interesting. I could have been the mysterious new guy that has everyone's attention. But no; I was the creepy, weird guy living in a fucking cleaning closet.

I sat back on my bed, shaking my head in disbelief when it hit me. What the fuck was I doing?

Volunteer

I was starting to regret coming here, but I was stuck. I couldn't go back with my tail between my legs, hoping Colin and Roisin had learnt their lesson with me leaving, I was too stubborn for that. I was here to prove a point. Equally, I couldn't just arrive here, offer my help and then leave, 'Oh hey Doctor Emmanuel, funny thing, I'm not actually supposed to be here. Got off a stop early, thanks for everything though'. I was going to have to stick it out for at least a week. Right now it was a bad dream, the opposite of what I hoped last night.

Alcohol was not a good assistant for giving advice or making decisions.

I knew the protocol for these situations; I had trained for such a scenario and had done the role-plays. We practiced for a lost team member rather than a deserter, naturally. Panic would ripple through the team, as I had experienced on a previous trip when we found out there was an ex junkie in the group. When he had alcohol he went into a blind rage, attacking himself and anyone who touched him, and eventually, we found him, heavily sedated in a Budapest hospital. Right about now, Colin and Roisin would be ringing my folks, and I would be better to pray for death out here than go home and face my mum, this was not a thing she would let go of lightly.

What would the team make of my sudden absence? Some would find it hilarious, though eventually, they would all come to hate me. Negativity would spread and any respect they had for me would be lost. Worse, if someone got seriously injured the medic would...oh no, he wouldn't be able to help because he was fuck knows where. Where was I anyway? The affiliates would be ringing around trying to find out my whereabouts, police would be involved, possibly even the British Consulate. Oh fuck! It dawned on me; I didn't even have my passport with me! I was screaming inside, but this was always my way, jumping in head first into the water without checking for rocks. Typical! I was floating down shit creek with a paddle, but no fucking canoe.

"Hello?" A young, black woman popped head around the door after knocking with a soft, almost fearful tap.

I guessed she was the nurse summoning me to come and do rounds. She wore the same style of head scarf as Odette, so it was more of a hospital thing like hair nets in a restaurant. I hoped I wouldn't have to wear one. She wore a uniform that identified her more readily as a nurse, a white long sleeve T-shirt, with three of four buttons on the front down from the neckline, sleeves rolled up to her elbows, and white loose fitted trousers.

It always puzzled me why they wore white; surely with the dust, blood and whatever else they encountered during the day, they would be a nightmare to clean. Nothing I had that was white ever stayed white.

"Come, come."

She waved her hand at me to follow her. This woman just about spoke English; it was going to be a long day.

I spent the first part of the afternoon following the nurse around with a trolley, dispensing slices of thinly-cut, crusty loaf that had been toasted on an open fire, then left to cool without butter. Wrong in my eyes, but I wasn't about to question the hospital's madness of butterless toast. I placed it into the hands of each patient, along with a small plastic cup filled with water, terrified I might spill it or split the cup. I was barely able to string two words together in Amharic. Handing over the water I said "Amesegënallô." I imagined how stupid that sounded - 'thank you for taking your water'. But the patients - mostly elderly with the odd new mother - grinned politely.

No sooner had we finished, then it was time to go around everyone again with my trusty trolley, which on occasions took a fit as the back right wheel shook violently, trying to break away from the other three. Attached to the handles, I had a blue bin liner for cleaning up, but there was no need for it as we left the cups to re-fill with water and there was never any food left. Those that didn't eat the toast saved it for whoever came to visit, not necessarily because they were hungry, but because they didn't like wasting food. Our tasks consisted of handing out medication and changing bandages. I stood beside the nurse holding whatever she needed, or at times played 'guess the object' as she pointed to items and laughed at my desperate attempts to understand what she wanted, lifting objects up or pointing to things until I got it right. She was polite and patient, I couldn't work out if she was just amused by the whole situation, or if she appreciated my enthusiasm. This took us well into the afternoon, and just when I thought I was done, I was called, by Emmanuel, to tend to a woman who needed a fresh set of bandages.

"You have gloves on?" he asked. I held up my hands to show them covered.

At the opposite end of the hospital from the reception was an entrance used for Accident and

Volunteer

Emergency, and the waiting room there had a few seats and a bed or two. I noticed a woman sitting by herself; the wrapping on her foot was disgusting. 'Please not her' I thought.

It was her.

I stared at Emmanuel in the hope he would point to someone else. I tried to be professional, but my body shuddered. I bent down, and coughed, nearly sick at the smell, using the muscles in my nose to close my nostrils as not to appear rude by covering my nose with a hand. Not that nearly coughing up and being sick over her was polite.

I didn't expect anything good to be uncovered from the bandages, but what was under them was horrendous. I sprang to my feet and gagged, forcing myself to cough to release the pressure in my chest and throat. I had tears in my eyes, trying not to throw up.

"It's leprosy. And before you panic, you won't catch it. Your health and years of vaccinations has made you immune. Most people here over the age of six are immune, unless they have had sexual relations with someone with leprosy, or were born with it."

"So, if you could put fresh bandages on and let this lady be on her way," he patted my back and nodded a smile to the woman.

Her smile was genuine. I politely returned it, covering my embarrassment and shame. But all the same, her foot was rotting away. It had a really deep purple-coloured bruise, curved like a 'C' around the outside of the foot and covering the toes. There was also a hint of brown inside the purple, and within the boundary lines was a pale greenish yellow.

Physically the foot was deformed as if it had been hit with a hammer numerous times, the big toe inflated, the toe next to it missing, the other three toes looked broken and pulled to the outside edge of the foot. Fresh cuts eaten into the foot were contrasted by a yellowing crust of hard skin that edged them. The wrapping had added a slight tinge of body odour to the air, but the overwhelming smell came from the foot itself. It smelt similar to sour milk, or vomit that had been left overnight.

I didn't know if she was in pain and was unable to ask her, even if I asked, I couldn't give her anything for it. My first aid course didn't cover leprosy. Electrocution yes, I could deal with that, but Leprosy and AIDs were a few grades higher. As much as I wanted to get this over, I took my time

Volunteer

and wrapped her foot with care, constantly checking if I was hurting her or if the wrapping was too tight. She smiled down at me, grateful for the attention and the help.

I stood up when finished, the woman stood up, too. She reached for my arm, I fought with myself not to move, but lost out to ignorance and I offered my hand instead, with the peace of mind that I had gloves on. Her wispy voice carried words I couldn't comprehend and she nodded continuously as I walked her to the door.

"Whoa! You forgot your shoes." I said, but she had no shoes. She stopped, trying to understand what I wanted. I hurried to open the door for her, pushed my back against it as she slid passed, still speaking softly and nodding her head. She patted my chest and crossed the dusty courtyard. So much for clean dressings, they would be stinking by the time she got to the main gate.

I guess this is how I envisioned Africa before coming here. It was a strange feeling being out of my depth, not being able to fully apply my first aid skills in this medical environment.

Was I better suited for social trips and one-off emergency situations, assisting a professional?

Gary McElkerney

Or was it simply that I struggled with the communication? Not so much out of my depth, but alone, doubting my abilities and falling at this first hurdle of a simple human interaction.

Chapter 12: Not Enough

The next few days followed the same routine in the morning, only my afternoon tasks changed. I had mopped the entire hospital corridor and toilet floors, and also spent an afternoon helping to vaccinate children, with what I didn't ask, but the needles were clean I knew that much as we ripped them out of plastic packaging. I was shown how to administer the injection, just like in the movies, wipe the skin with cotton wool that was soaked in surgical spirits, slowly insert the needle, inject the drug, pull it back out and hold the cotton ball in place then get the mother to hold it. The nurse would speak to the mother or guardian, get an answer, write something down and hand out a small slip of paper - Next.

I helped to rebuild a wall that a delivery driver had demolished some time ago, and that had slowly disintegrated to mounds of rubble in parts. I knocked down the remaining wall, which dissolved at the slightest touch, the red clay bricks crumbled

Gary McElkerney

like a drowning sand castle. All that remained strong was the foot-wide strip of cement that ran the full length of the hospital making my job easier from the abandoned pile of breeze-blocks that sat at the back of the clinic I built a new wall. The breeze-blocks were different to the ones back home. These were hollow, like an extruded calculator number '8', about a foot long, and half a foot wide as it were high. Heavy too. They broke quite easily, demonstrated by my careless grip on one dropping it from knee height.

I had already learnt that in this country you needed to be educated quickly by your mistakes and I was never slow to pick up something new. I mixed the cement and sand with water, a technique I'd learned from building the medical clinic in Nicaragua and carefully scooped it into a black bucket. I threw some of it in place, and then carefully lined up the breeze blocks, following the line of string tied to wooden posts along the concrete strip. Genius technique from Negasi for getting a straight line.

While my preparation was spot on, my application was not. This was Ethiopia, it was warm and cement mix here dried faster than anywhere else on earth. Fact. I was chipping off the old concrete mix so I could put the next few blocks down straight, and the remaining cement mix in the bucket hardened. Shaking my fists to the heavens with a cry of 'why?' with some notion I would get an answer, I hammered the sides of the bucket to break up its contents. Not being so patient in these matters, gentle hammering was never going to be an option, and the bucket shattered around its concrete filling.

"Fuck!" I screamed. The one word in the English language that fitted any context. Only five blocks had been put into place and the rest of the cement mix I had made had hardened too. Half a bag of sand and cement wasted on five blocks. Employee of the year, I was not.

Like I said, I learn quickly, and working alone I kept the mixes small and worked fast, laying down 150 blocks that day. My arms hung like lead weights from my shoulders and later I collapsed on my bed to rest for a few minutes, but didn't surface until the next morning.

The following day the onslaught continued. Lunch was basic; rice and beans - two foods I can no longer stomach, at least not in the same meal. I ate as I set up, washing it down with a bottle of water, part of my four litres a day, which probably wasn't enough, but why waste water when there was plenty of beer in the world. Fluids were a necessity, but was it really too much to ask for diluted juice at least?

I was tasked to dig out a large hole and support the perimeter of it with more breeze-blocks, which seemed to have appeared overnight. I had no idea what it would be used for, but I would dig without question. Thanks to my previous experience, digging a hole wasn't a problem, I was used to digging foundations so I was quickly near the depth I needed to be. My enthusiasm confirmed the notion that I was as happy as a pig in shit flinging dirt carelessly out of the hole to Odette's amusement on her smoke breaks.

I had been betrayed by my own ideas of adventure; I didn't sign up for this. Well, I did, but building houses back in Dessie with the team was more exciting than this. OK, so we had a few emergencies brought in over the last day or two, but I wanted to be part of that rush, to make a difference in the field, not be stuck in a hole with a shovel and the occasional visit from Odette bringing water and giving a nod of approval at my progress.

I had yet to have a meaningful conversation with Odette. I tried to think of a question or something to comment on.

Volunteer

There had to be more than this.

I don't base my life on the idea that everything happens for a reason, or hand of God coincidences like my mum, but I couldn't have timed my thoughts any better.

At that moment, two MAA 4x4 pick-ups raced through the main gate and sprayed the building with stones and dust as they screeched to a halt and skidded. They were still moving as doors were flung open and bodies jumped out and raced to the back of the vehicles.

Emmanuel burst out from the clinic,

"Christophe!" He shouted, waving his hand beckoning me to the 4x4s. Could you have stopped me? I was out of that hole like a shot, across the loose gravel, kicking half of my work back in the hole thinking 'you only see this on television'.

"Quick Christophe, bring them into the first two rooms!" Emmanuel instructed. I nodded as I helped to lift a stretcher off the back of the pick-up.

A young girl unconscious, was covered over with a thin, olive-green blanket and we half ran with her across the yard and through the metal doors. We followed the shouts down the corridor into the first of the rooms, passing two nurses who herded us in and took her to an empty bed. The blanket was pulled off her as she was slid onto the bed and I stood awkwardly waiting for further instructions

A young, black doctor went over her vital signs, with me checking through them in my head and remembering each stage as he did it. I needed one of those lights to shine in people's eyes. The child was breathing, that was good enough for me. She wore a pink floral dress with intricate off white patterned collar, and a belt. The dress was too big, like she had been playing 'dress-up' and the belt was the only thing that kept it on her. I imagined her adjusting it up around her tiny shoulders time and again. The dress was pulled up on one side and covered in blood, part torn, part burnt. She only had one sandal on her left foot while her right leg was loosely bandaged from the ankle to half way up her thigh. Her right forearm was bandaged and there was a square patch on her cheek. All had the rusted look of blood, seeping through them.

Eventually, I focused, sensing the urgency and panic in the room as I was shifted around the bed, more of a hindrance, but I wanted to help. I stood silently waiting for instructions, my sub conscious screamed and waved frantically.

Volunteer

Then, the American entered. At the risk of being racist was it better to say half-caste? Or Black, or African-American? Not sure what was more offensive, pointing out that you're not native to America or the focus being colour. To me an American was an American, regardless of skin colour. He didn't have a southern state accent like George Bush's or a hillbilly accent, so was he from one of the northern states? I was useless with accents.

"Hey! Give us a hand here man. What's your name?" He asked.

"Chris"

"Cool, I'm Michael." He said, placing a hand on his chest.

"I need you to give me a hand, take some wrapping and spread it out over the beds. See if the other guys need a hand and if not come see me by the trucks."

I took the wrapping and ran to the other room, placing two wraps on each bed. No one noticed me, or shouted for help, so I went to find Michael.

He was the same height as me, a larger build with black hair cut close to his head. Dressed in a black T-shirt a size too big, a pair of camouflaged shorts and combat boots and had the 'too cool for school' image as he stood on the back of one of the pick-up trucks.

"Can you throw some of that water in here," he asked, "and pour the rest into the other truck? Cheers. You're Scottish I take it?"

"Northern Irish." I poured the water into the blood soaked trailer and moved to the other and did the same.

"Sorry. My bad. You been here long? You a nurse?" Normally I would have taken the opportunity to woo this guy over with my Northern Irish charm, but the sudden burst of adrenaline had drained me, and this guy was too cool. He'd have sniffed out my bullshit no problem.

"No. I arrived three days ago from Dessie. Was working down there, but heard they needed help up here. Just been labouring and helping the nurses. That's about it really, nothing exciting."

I got up on the back of the other pick up and pushed the diluted blood and dirt off the back with a brush, fighting with blood trying to make its way back towards the cab. There was a lot of blood here, but I wasn't sickened or freaked out.

Volunteer

"That's pretty shit. Man, you need to be out with us. White guy like you is fucking gold dust up at the front, plus it beats nurse duties."

He watched me meticulously trying to brush out every groove. "Hey, don't be precious about getting that clean, quick brush will do it."

"So, why does being white make me gold dust and what front you talking about? I thought the war was over years ago?"

Michael sat on the side of the truck.

"Agreements were signed by the politicians who all benefited from it, but the die-hard rebels like the LF – the Liberation Front, that is," he explained, "are pushing their luck with the border. They believe that some of the villages in Ethiopia belong to them, particularly in the northwest up around Badme. They creep across and wreak fucking havoc, hitting military targets, Ethiopian businesses, transports and shit. But it's always the innocent people who get fucked. So, we head for the smoke, pick up the injured and take them to the nearest clinic, usually this one. It's the best of a bad bunch."

"Like paramedics?" My eyes widened.

This was it. This was what I wanted. I sat on the side of the 4x4, mimicking Michael, my legs dangling down the side of the wheel arch with heels resting on the tyre for stability, as if this was how I customarily sat on a truck.

"Yeah, I guess we are. You're gold dust 'cause as soon as your ass is there, the rebels will pull out. You could be a journalist, or a doctor from an agency. They can't risk cutting you down."

I was confused, trying to figure out if this was a racist jab. I'd never really been racially abused, apart from one time in Nicaragua when a local threw his apple core at me from across the street calling me a *Gringo*. But that didn't really bother me; I wasn't going to be working there long enough to care. I'd soon be headed home to hot showers, a fridge full of food and a comfortable bed. That leather-faced man, whose hard life had taken a toll on him physically, may have had all of the above as well.

"Look it's almost common sense. They have an objective, and as it stands, the odds aren't in their favour. But it could be worse. They can shoot as many Ethiopians and blacks as they want, and no one barely bats an eyelid. 'Cause Fuck, this is Africa! But if a white aid worker gets killed or murdered it's a global fucking tragedy. Enquiries

Volunteer

are started, UN Peacekeeping Forces are thrown in, sanctions are made, aid is pulled, because war means refugees, and that's a different matter entirely. No one wants another country's war castoffs sponging their limited resources. It isn't worth it."

"Hold on, you're black, but you're not from here, right? Surely they aren't going to shoot you, you're no different from me? You're American and it doesn't take much for Americans to want to kick the ass out of people. No offence." I was confused by this apparent racial line being drawn up.

"Not to be racist here, but you're White. I'm Black. I look no different from the rest of them. How would they know they were shooting an American, until it was too late?" Michael explained. "So, what do you say? You in?"

I was feeling some loyalty to Emmanuel and the clinic; ironic since a few days ago I upped and left the team I came out with. But I wanted this. I believed this was my calling. Or I told myself that as a way of justifying running out on the clinic.

"Yeah I guess. Why not, if I'm needed?"

Talking to Emmanuel, though, was the problem. I didn't think leaving to help these guys would be the issue. The issue was me having the balls to ask. I hated having to talk to people about awkward topics.

"Awesome, I'll talk to the big man. You get your shit together, we set off first thing tomorrow."

So that clinched it. I was elated, I couldn't wait to tell people back home that, not only was I working as part of a paramedic crew, I was going to war! I probably wouldn't see any action, but who knows? Regardless, I was going to be part of something big. Adrenaline was pumping as I raced into the clinic up the stairs, clearing two, then three steps at a time and ran down the corridor at pace that caused a nurse to freeze up against a wall. I packed my stuff which I could have done in five minutes tomorrow morning, but I was too excited for that.

Technically, I wasn't leaving the clinic. My role was changing, I'd just moved departments. What was I going to do; carry all my crap about? Sure, you never know when you're going to need your wash bag. Shaking my head, I emptied the bundled mess onto the bed, throwing the bag onto the floor and sat on the bed. Staring at the pile, I realised I had nothing to wear in the way of protection. Was Michael wearing a vest? Was there any protective gear on 4x4s? Oh shit.

Chapter 13: Naive

The morning finally dawned. I hadn't really slept, just drifted in and out of sleep, afraid I would miss the first day of my life changing experience. Michael slapped the back of my door then burst into the room.

"It's your morning wake-up call, Sunshine. I know it's early, but get your shit together, we've got to move!" I bounced off the bed and pulled on my washed-out combats. I was going to the frontline after all, so I needed to look the part. What would I need? Sun cream, small personal medical pack, raincoat, cap, camera, book? Extra socks? I threw what I needed in to a bag and pushed on my boots.

As I jogged down the corridor, I pulled my T-shirt on, stretching it over my head with one hand, my bag in the other hand. There was a cool breeze in the corridor which blew across my stomach. Outside I could hear the commotion, noise from the engines of the 4x4s already running. I broke into a jog down the stairs, trying not to step on my laces, when it would probably have been easier to stop and tie them. I got to the bottom of the stairs and froze. Odette was in Michael's arms. A dull ache of disappointment formed in my gut. The same feeling of regret you get from not having the nerve to speak to that girl in the bar and you watch her leave your life forever. What would I do anyway? Even if I was given a chance I would still fuck it up.

"There he is. You ready?" Michael was proud of his new recruit.

"Yeah, let's do this." I nodded stiffly to Odette on the walk past.

"Hey!" She pulled me to her. I hesitated, and then slid into her welcoming arms, wrapping my own around her in a tight hug.

"Stay safe. Don't try to be a hero. It doesn't always pay off," she whispered.

"Ok." With a nod, I followed Michael to the truck, throwing my bag into the back seat alongside the medical supplies and I jumped on to the open back with three other guys. Here I was; the big shot. We were like heroes in some American war movie, getting ready to hit the frontline. All we needed was

Volunteer

the theme music. We drove away from the clinic, Odette waved to us. This was it.

A distress call had come in on the clinic's communications radio. A bus station nearby had been hit, and fighting had spread out over one of the local towns with the rebels using hit and run guerrilla tactics. Getting close with the 4x4s would be an issue, so we would go in on foot, that way we would be a smaller target. I was pumped. Cool air hit my face as we sped along the dusty road under another bright sky. This was one of the moments that can still catch me off guard now and again, a flashback that seems to freeze in time whenever I see any blue sky now.

"Do we have protective combat gear?" I shouted over the noise of the engine and the wind to Michael, who sat opposite me on the back of the pickup.

"Yeah, of course!" Michael shouted back.

"Good! I was worried because I don't have any with me!" I never expected to be doing this so why would I have them. Michael laughed, shaking his head.

"Fuck man! You serious? No we don't. We're not soldiers. We don't have headgear, or body armour. There is no emergency evac. This isn't the army. If you're in the shit, you're in shit. You do what you have to and get out because in the end man, out here you don't get to choose whether you live or die!"

We drove for the next half an hour in silence. It was useless to try to say anything over the noise of the wind. For me I was bursting to say something, almost jumping up and down like an eager child. I had no idea what we were driving in to, at the same time I was uneasy with the lack of protection.

My mind was constructing scenarios, building up scenes in my head, piecing together images from the news, films and games. I had notions of greatness, sadness, and heroism. I had only dreamt of moments like this, the day I would be called on to do my part, my scene was set, my theme music was the engine sounds and the air roaring past my ears. Finally, the silence was broken.

"We got smoke!" Michael shouted, pointing towards it.

A large plume, thick and black tumbled into the air. Smaller grey spirals wisped close to it. There was crackling; sporadic across the town and before I

Volunteer

could work out where it was coming from the next burst went off. There was so much to take in that I took in nothing.

The truck skidded into action and everyone bailed out. Michael pointed and screamed out orders. It was chaos. People ran by, wailing. Two cars were burning on the opposite side of the road. A building on fire, people dragging fuck knows what, through the street. Possessions or looting? Some were carrying other people.

Where was the medical post? Where the fuck was the Red Cross, or the UN tents and medical supplies? I had pictured the frontline war scene in my head, running through trenches with an innocent civilian on my back, but that was just daydreaming. I never expected it would happen. I wasn't trained for this. I couldn't do this. My body shuddered at a distant explosion, it could have been a toilet seat falling, or a dodgy car exhaust for all I knew, but everything was magnified and getting blown out of proportion. I should have stayed at the clinic.

"Chris, let's go, you're with me!" Michael called out, waving me to him.

Then it hit me. My breathing became urgent, my heart raced and it felt as if my insides had fallen out through my ass. Maybe it was shock, but more likely it was pure fear. My ego screamed 'Go! Go! Go!' as if a physical being inside my head was trying to take the lead, pushing me on. But the harder it urged, the tighter my fingers gripped the edge of the 4x4. I was going to die. I was on the verge of pissing myself; I tightened my abdomen to hold it in. I felt sick, my heart pounded in my throat.

"Chris, let's go! Get off the fucking truck! And grab that bag!" Michael demanded with his hand stretched out towards me, his eyes directed somewhere else. Fear pinned me to the 4x4. A form of terror-fuelled Tourette's had me shaking my head and stuttering words as an excuse.

"I...I can't!" I screamed. Michael spun mid-conversation with someone, to glare at me.

"Fuck man! You better be shitting me! You need to sort your shit out now! Get off the God damn truck!"

I dropped my head to hide my shame, but it was on show for everyone as the words 'I can't' fell out of my mouth, picked up by the short bursts of air pushed from my lungs. Michael shook his head in disbelief, and disappointment, as he reached in and snatched the medical bag out of the 4x4.

Volunteer

"Fuck! Fine. You need to deal with whatever comes to the trucks. Jesus!"

With that, Michael took off around the corner of a building and I was alone with the chaos.

I tried to block out the noise, closing my eyes and tightening my grip on the 4x4. I fought to control my lungs and my composure; I could do this. No, I couldn't. I stamped down hard with my foot.

"Fuck!" I screamed.

I said it again. "Fuck."

Quieter. Disappointed.

I was exhausted and deflated, gone were the dreams of being a hero, telling my war stories, moments of daydreaming becoming reality. It wasn't about the difference I would make to those I would save. Fuck that. It was about the difference it would make for me. Stepping up, convincing everyone that I was more than what I really was and being admired for it.

Of all the shit that had happened in my life, this was supposed to be my time, my moment. I was supposed to either return alive a hero - or die a heroic death. Instead, I was a stuttering, shaking coward, who had almost pissed himself.

This was my reality.

I was nothing back home for this reason. Living with my parents and newly single, I was a pathetic, four-eyed recluse. Bullied when I was at school because I was too much of a coward to stick up for myself. This was all I was ever going to be. Everything I had trained for, everything I had worked for, gone to shit in this moment.

Tears of self-pity threatened to overflow, when a man staggered towards me, a body bundled on his back. It was one of the guys from the other 4x4 and he called for me to help. I wiped the unbroken tears from my eyes and sniffed, then grabbed a medical bag and jumped off the truck. I rushed to him as he dropped to his knees and slid the man onto the ground. Pulling on my gloves I examined the casualty. He was conscious, but clearly in shock and not responding too well. Warmth spread across my stomach and, thinking I had finally pissed myself, I looked down. It was blood; a lot of blood.

This man had lost an arm and his blood was streaming out of the wound, over me. I slapped my

Volunteer

forehead. How had I had missed something as obvious as that? I grabbed a bandage from the medical bag, cut off a length, and tied it above the injury, then frantically wrapped around the stump what was left. There was nothing professional about it. Still, I got it on and tied it up, all the while the blood soaking through. I lifted his legs, with the other volunteer carrying his upper body, and we awkwardly transferred him to the 4x4.

I hadn't noticed that Michael was standing by the other 4x4 with a woman he had brought back. "Good to see you grew a set and got a grip on reality. You pull that shit tomorrow I'll trade you in for someone who will actually be of use. We'll just call this a first day minor freak out. Take over for me here; I'm headed to the bus station."

I jumped off the back of the truck and got to work.

Chapter 14: Adrenaline Rush

Next day we headed off first thing again, down the same road, this time to a neighbouring town a few miles from the one we were at yesterday.

It was much the same type of radio call, a rebel attack, and this time in a residential area close to a police training base. The wake-up call was the same, the preparation was the same, and Odette, ever faithful, was at the bottom of the stairs for the goodbye hug and inspirational 'quote of the day'.

"There is no shame in being afraid, better to be afraid and stay safe than to die out there alone," she whispered.

Where did she get this from and why the obsession with death? Did she know something I didn't? I nodded and she handed me two rounds of toast and an apple. I juggled with my bag trying to open the zip on the smallest front pocket to put in the apple, Odette holding out a plastic bottle that I hoped was tea.

"It's tea. There is no sugar though, but should get you started."

"Thank you." I held up the tea, signalling my thanks. It was strange drinking warm tea out of a plastic bottle, but welcomed.

"You'll be fine," she assured me.

Shit, she had heard about yesterday. Fucking brilliant; she was the last person I had wanted to know. I walked on, embarrassed, acting as if it hadn't fazed me. I wanted to believe her, that I would be fine, but truth be told, I hadn't slept much with the worry of it.

I threw my bag into the back of the 4x4 and took my seat on the pickup opposite Michael. I stood up as we moved off to take my iPod out of my back pocket unwinding the white earphones from around the thin black sleeve that it was clothed in, and placed them in my ears.

As we headed off, I knew Odette was waving at me, but I pretended not to pay attention, but the whole time I knew I was being watched, but I tried not to notice, or care. I turned on the iPod and rotated my thumb over the grey click wheel to 'Artist: Samuel Barber, Song: Adagio for Strings, Repeat.' I slid the iPod back into its sleeve and I buttoned it into my side leg pocket.

This song popped up randomly in my life and soon became an anthem to my troubled mind. The strings helped align my thoughts and made sense of them. I had run the events and failures of my life over and over in my head, mixing reality with imaginings of 'What if?' But the issue wasn't what I could have done, it was why I didn't. I feared death. Had I been kidding myself that I was cut out for this? There had to be more than, well, this. More to me. More than the disappointing persona I had carried so far in my life. Maybe I would always feel I had fallen short, yet I had achieved so much in my life, more than most, but I wanted more.

Again, it was a quiet drive, but the atmosphere didn't feel the same as yesterday. Maybe I was being paranoid, but I thought it was due to my 'freak out', as we were calling it and I found myself trying to catch the stares of the other guys. I attempted to distract myself by changing the song on the iPod to 'Children' by Robert Miles; the first single I had ever bought with my own money, at the age of fourteen on tape cassette, no less. Dropping my head back staring at the clear blue sky,

Volunteer

I tried to overcome my paranoia, and keep my nerves in check. I had to do this; no more bullshit. And so the smoke came into view.

We drove deeper into the town. An army patrol on the road behind us had split our convoy up, with all the medical equipment in the other 4x4. That gave me some time to get my ass in gear, and nerves in check before we arrived. The town didn't seem that big, but I had only driven down a few streets so how the hell would I know? We might have been at the far side already, or an hour away from the incident. We pulled into a car park outside a block of flats and some distance from the sounds of shooting and small explosions.

"Chris, get your shit together and do what you have to, but when our other truck gets here we're going to work. That or I'll trail you off the fucking truck myself!" Michael ordered. I nodded with a false sense of confidence, familiar fingers of panic waved inside me. My body shook, but I had to get involved today, no matter what. Whether Michael's threat was genuine or not, if I didn't get off this truck today I would be brushing out the clinic for the rest of my stay. Only one military 4x4 was on its way down the road followed by our MAA truck. All the 4x4s were the same out here, only the paint work and company branding differed one from another. There was at least three military 4x4s, why was one still escorting ours?

Michael attended a young mother with a child in her arms, who was shouting in a pleading manner. Either she was failing to get her point across or wasn't getting the answer she wanted. The child was barely hanging onto her neck, almost falling backwards over her arm, screaming. The mother demanded Michael do something, directing his attention to the smoke four hundred metres away. The flash came first; there was a pause and then a bang, which was enough for me to dive out of the 4x4 in panic.

The explosion made everyone jump, but only I over-reacted. The military truck that was escorting our other 4x4 had been hit, its back-end shredded and twisted. The truck swung to the right, then to the left before flipping over and rolling, flinging its human contents lifelessly through the air. Our 4x4, driving behind, crashed into the tumbling mess and skidded to a halt. As the dust settled there was a terrified silence before screams poured from the MAA 4x4, our guys rolled off the back and staggered about. From the military truck there was deathly tranquillity. I didn't know how to react. On one hand, it had the captivating effect of an amazing

Volunteer

action scene from a movie. On the other, this was horrifyingly real, and much too close for comfort.

"Fuck me! Chris, can you drive?" Michael shouted, pointing at me, as he abandoned the woman and her child.

"I don't have a license."

"It's an automatic, like dodgems. Just push the accelerator, pedal, and steer, but try not to hit anything. Get to the truck and get everyone in it. Bring it back here," he ordered.

"What? I can't! Are you blind? They're blowing the shit out of the 4x4s!" Our driver was fine - why not fucking send him?

"Chris. Shut the fuck up and get the fucking truck! You're the only one who can, and you know why. That's our guys Chris, and they need help! They are our guys! Go get our guys!" He stood pointing with urgency, towards the crash.

"Fuck!" I shouted. I pulled myself to my feet and pushed off the end of the truck.

Back in senior school I was a long distance runner, not a sprinter, but Linford Christie had nothing on me right then. My arms and legs pumped as I ran with the fear of God. Faster than I had ever run before, I charged down the street, like a toddler about to fall over themselves because their legs couldn't keep up. Every footstep shuddered through my body as I dropped my head, believing I would get there quicker. It was the longest four hundred metres I had ever run.

"Get in!" I screamed at the volunteers lying on the ground. I reached the driver's door and flung it open, glass from the windscreen spilled onto the ground.

"Move over!" I pushed my way into the driver's seat and slammed the door behind me. Desperately, I fiddled with the keys and they fell out of the ignition and through my fingers.

"Fuck!" My panic and frustration was evident and the screaming wasn't helping. The key had already been in the slot, all I had to do was turn it. How the fuck did I manage to drop the keys?

"Move! Move! Move!" I rummaged on the floor for the keys, pushing legs out of the way without care. Got them! I slammed the key straight into the ignition; the engine coughed, but refused to endure more agony. I turned the key again. If it didn't fire up this time, I was out of there. I had already spent too long here, convinced I was being lined up in the sights of another RPG, or missile, or whatever the fuck they were blowing shit up with. I pushed the gear stick into 'P' and the engine roared. I slammed my foot on the accelerator and the truck lifted without going anywhere. This wasn't like dodgems. I slapped my hand onto the steering wheel. I turned to my passenger; his face was covered in blood, either from where the windscreen had blown through with the explosion, or from the impact with the military 4x4. He in turn was holding onto the driver, who was unconscious, but then you would be if you head-butted the steering wheel hard enough to split your head open.

"How does this work?" He leaned across and with a bloodied hand slapped the gear stick and pointed to the 'R'. R for reverse. Obvious; I needed to think straight. I threw the 4x4 back from the smoking mess and slammed on the brake.

"Now what?" I was desperate and he pointed, this time to the 'D'. Without hesitation, I stomped on the accelerator and propelled us along the road, expecting a missile to flip us as we passed the top of every street. Terror had me convinced, rightly or wrongly, that the gunfire and explosions were getting closer. I was sure I drove part of the way with my eyes closed, visions of me falling out of the 4x4 in flames after an RPG attack danced in my head. Pulling up beside the other 4x4, I slammed again on the brake. There was a thud of bodies as we came to a sudden stop.

"Sorry!" I yelled, and jumped out of the driver's seat, relieved to be out of the truck. I was going to have a panic attack and really wanted to throw up.

Michael directed the other volunteers to look after the crew.

"You're with me!" He said, as he threw one of the medical bags my way. My breath was short and heavy, sweat dripped down my lower back, and my twisted T-shirt was stuck to my shoulders.

"Let's go."

Michael ran through an archway into a residential compound, racing across the courtyard as I dragged myself after him. Was all right for him, but I needed a break. Emotional and physical exhaustion had me gripped and there was no energy left to keep this up. I shuffled after him, my mind was working overtime; I needed a gun, a vest and a helmet. I searched for scoping eyes watching from cracks in walls, doors and windows. Everyone had locked themselves indoors, but the action was too

Volunteer

much to not be curious. I crept across the courtyard and my body tightened as I waited for a sniper to hit me from the shadows and leave me to bleed out in plain sight of everyone. It never came. Too busy wrapped up in my over-active imagination, I ran into the back of Michael who had stopped at a corner.

"Whoa whoa!" He patted the air with his hand, motioning for me to stay behind him, which I had no problem with. If he wanted to be a human shield that was fine with me.

"What is it?" I enquired.

"Nothing. Just thinking."

"Any fucking chance you can think some other time and place?" I pleaded.

"Calm down. Police station - or just scope around the town? We might run into rebels, or crossfire. Hmmm."

"Preferably the one that has the least likelihood of us running into to the LF." I did not want to be hanging about. It was uncomfortably quiet and we all know from the movies what happens when it's too quiet.

"OK. Police station it is." Michael decided. He moved down the street with me behind him, I was bent over taking quick small steps, my left hand brushing the walls as if I was running blind, using them as a guide and to keep my balance. A few buildings down we came to one with a long porch. Michael stopped and rested on one knee, I copied his stance while he gave the instructions.

"OK, at the bottom of the street, you see the wall?" He pointed and I nodded, hoping we were talking about the same wall. "We go over that wall then run left along it. That takes us up to the police station. Smoke will give it away, but just follow me anyway."

His breathing was heavy, not because he was unfit; he appeared fitter than me and I was naturally athletic, it was the heat and nerves. He never showed any fear, but he had to be a little anxious.

"When I say move, we move," he said.

Why were we waiting? I twitched to get going. The street was empty. Was there a vehicle coming? Did he see or hear something I didn't?

I heard nothing, but distant gunfire. We needed to move before my mind engineered its own version of what was going to happen.

Volunteer

"Move."

We both set off, hearing the spitting sound of gunfire and bursts of explosion in the distance. I was aware of my breathing, time slowed to its rhythm and everything else faded. I left Michael eating my dust as I sprinted for my life, the wall at the end of the street being my only objective. But it wasn't long before I redirected my focus to the gunfire and explosions, and bullets fizzing through the air around us. I broke my stride into stuttering steps, lifting my arms up around my head and contemplated dropping to the ground and rolling up into a ball.

Where the hell was it coming from? Was it friendly fire? When was being shot at ever friendly?

I got back into my sprint, powered by desperation and panic, my arms twitching towards my head as I altered my line of running with every noise that broke the air. As I approached the wall, I half thought of jumping clean over it, or taking it in a Hollywood roll, but wimped out at the last second and slid up it, awkwardly throwing one leg up and swung the other over. There could have been a six-foot drop behind that wall, I was just being sensible.

I dropped to the ground into a crouched position, and then jumped back from the muffled scream of a woman, who was holding a child to her chest, covering its ears. Was it the same woman Michael had spoken to at the 4x4? Not possible, idiot. How the hell would she have got here quicker than us? Michael came over the wall soon after and slapped my chest to follow him. The child looked at me from its mother's arms. I gave it a 'thumbs up'. What else could I do?

We kept our heads lower than the top of the wall and shuffled along it, almost on all fours at times, until we came to the end.

"That's the police station fence," Michael said. "We go up to the left and the entrance should be there on the right, across the street."

"Should be?" I enquired. Right now I needed certainty not guesses.

"Yeah I'm pretty sure, let's go."

As we ran across the street I dared not look up for fear I would attract attention. If I was going to get hit, I didn't want to see it coming. I continued to run, keeping low to the ground until I reached the entrance of the police station courtyard.

Volunteer

In the courtyard was an empty military truck that I assumed belonged to the Ethiopian Army, who were holding back the rebels further up the town. Two police 4x4s were on fire and the one storey office had flames flickering inside. All the windows were blown out and two police officers stood dressed in blue shirts that were splattered with blood, one wearing a navy beret, both were carrying AK47s and looked shocked and lost.

"Check him!" Michael pointed to a body close to the gate that I had run passed. I rolled the bloodied body of the policeman over, to check for a pulse, not that there was much point. He had been shot a few times in the chest and neck. Blood had covered the front of his shirt and he had been dead a while. I let go and he rolled back, face down into the dust. The stain of dried blood served as a chalk outline.

"He's dead," I said, running back to Michael, who was talking to the police officers, and tending to an injured man on the floor.

"Turns out the fighting isn't too bad where we came in, so you take this guy and head back to the trucks the way we came."

"Hold on what? I've got to carry him back by myself?" I knew this was how things were done.

I'd seen the guys coming back with casualties the day before, but I didn't think I could carry him the distance.

"Yeah, throw him over your shoulder, or on your back, whatever works for you. Go. I'll see you back at the trucks. If you run into shit, lay low and move when it's safe." Michael lifted the man's arm and I moved in to lift the other and pull him up on to his feet.

"Who is he?" I was trying to work out how I was going to carry this man back.

"It doesn't matter who he is. He's just a civilian, injured in the crossfire and these guys pulled him in here. Good luck and remember keep low." I threw the newly bandaged, semi-conscious man onto my back. He had a leg wound that I guessed was from a bullet and half his face was taped up. I ran through the gate and when I say ran, I mean with quick little steps, occasionally stopping to bounce the guy into a better position.

Although he was conscious and muttering to himself he wasn't able to help me at all. A complete rag doll on my back. It also didn't help that I was conscious of everything else bar what I was actually supposed to be doing. I was aware of the sun beating

Volunteer

down on us, of my sweat soaked back, most of it from my passenger. I looked at his arm dangling in front of me; beads of perspiration ran around the black hairs on his arm and dripped down his hand, along one of his fingers. I noticed the blood stain that had come from his leg, had spread over his washed-out brown trousers and was being absorbed by my combats. As gravity would have it, this blood stain transfer was making its way down to the ground, via my trousers. I wanted to drop him, but if he was fully conscious he would have got off.

I am sure this human taxi ride, in the form of a degrading piggy back, was no first class service for him, with the pain he was already suffering. In all, the trip back was taking too long and my freak out moments weren't helping. As soon as I heard a sudden blast or gunfire, I bolted for the nearest wall, slamming against it, waiting a while before checking that the coast was clear and moving on.

Shit - I was lost. I stopped in the middle of the road, desperate for a glimpse of Michael, the 4x4s or something familiar. I was always great with directions, but as I looked left and right there was nothing triggering a memory. Was it the street I passed, or was it the next street up? Fuck. I took steps back and forth, towards each street before choosing the street I had just passed. I picked up the pace out of desperation, wincing at the sweat dripping into my eyes.

I was panicking, but doing my utmost to convince my passenger that I knew fine rightly where I was going. I reached up to adjust my hat, that was making my forehead itch, and the weight on my back shifted. I don't know at what stage I realised what had happened. At first, I thought he was falling off, or that I had lost my footing and we were both going down. I tried to see what I was tripping on, but the speed we were going down suggested otherwise. I would usually have enough time to adjust my feet and catch myself if I had tripped, but I went straight down.

As I fell, it never occurred to me to let the man on my back go, so I could use my hands to save myself. Instead, my grip on his thighs tightened as I went down onto my right knee and rolled onto my side. I landed on top of my casualty, leaving me face up. Embarrassed, I sprang to my feet, and came face to face with a grinning LF rebel.

"Motherfucker!"

I stood, acting the typical Northern Irish hard man; chest out, with a stare that said I was ready to kill or be killed, my muscles pulsing in my jawbone.

Volunteer

The rebel was about the same age as me, shirtless with a baseball cap placed backwards on his head. Behind him, was another rebel, also grinning, wearing a straw hat and a waistcoat. As ridiculous as he looked, I fought against mocking his lack of style and fashion sense. My expression remained steadfast. The rebel had kicked or pushed at the injured man on my back, causing us to fall, and now he shouted at him. Both of the rebels laughed, while I shook with anger, but I was outnumbered and outgunned. I don't know if it was instinct or adrenaline, but I was ready to fight for our lives and I took stock of where his gun was, not that I knew what to do if I got a hold of it.

He directed his attention to me, pushing his face closer to mine and he muttered something, which I knew by his expression was an insult, or something condescending, his whispered tone dripped with pure hate from every word as he passed me. Now, I don't know where I got a set of balls from, but I stepped sideward and blocked his path, and in a low tone I reciprocated the threat, right in to his face.

"I don't fucking think so," I growled.

Suddenly, the straw-hatted rebel, who had being playing look out, tapped his comrade's shoulder with urgency, motioning that they had to leave. He shrugged, disgusted at losing the opportunity to have a go at me, and glared. I braced myself, convinced he was about to swing for me and we stood motionless for a few seconds before he spat on my shoes, and then strode off muttering at the ground, refusing to make eye contact. I shook so violently that I was unable to move, and as my muscles relaxed, I wasn't sure whether I would collapse from overdosing on adrenaline or from forgetting to breathe. Even so, I wanted to run after them. To do what, I had no idea. My patient hadn't moved an inch during the encounter and I motioned for him to give me his hand so I could pick him up. He nodded, grateful that I had stood up for him.

Not sure if I did it for him. Not sure why I did it at all.

Chapter 15: Hell Hole

We loaded up the 4x4s with the injured and they pulled away.

"Whoa! What about us?" I exclaimed, flapping my arms in the air at the driver. I hoped it was just an oversight that he hadn't waited for us to hop on board. He didn't stop.

"Stop freaking out. We're heading to the Hell Hole." Michael lifted his bag and set off with the same urgency as before. Now why on earth would I want to go to a place called 'The Hell Hole'? Spa treatment, was it? A pool with a bar at a private club, maybe? Here? Not a chance it was anything like that. Nothing with that name was going to be good out here, but I didn't have an alternative. Michael and the guys weren't stupid and I wasn't about to stay here alone, wherever here was.

Gary McElkerney

We walked over a mile across the town and had I known what a potential suicide mission it was to get to this 'Hell Hole' I would have stayed put. The start of the journey was grand, we ran through small back streets and courtyards, with Michael leading, another aid worker ahead of me, Alem, or maybe Alan, or Adam or something, then me, then another guy I didn't know, in fact, this was the first time I'd laid eyes on him. Maybe after the incident this morning they had called in a new set of aid workers, like reserves. I was guessing, but either way he was watching my back, and by that I mean I would hear him getting shot before I was.

When we reached the main streets we ran out between the firing lines, straight across to save time and get to the destination as fast as we could. This was not good when fear brought on my 'headless chicken' syndrome. I had been scared before, but never to the point that I was convinced we were going to die. Christ, there was even the odd body in the street, which validated the fear.

Despite that, I continued to make darting runs through the streets, while bullets flew around us, sending out warning puffs of dust when they pinged off buildings and anything else in the street, letting us know we'd been spotted.

Volunteer

Our only relief became the small alleyways between the main streets, but we didn't stop to take refuge there, or even to catch our breath. The guys weren't prepared to tempt fate in the open and we charged across a smoke-filled street. I relaxed; this street was quiet and empty. Just as I thought that, a crack fractured the silence and the corner of the wall exploded into my face.

"Ah. Fuck!" I screamed, forcing the edges of my palms into my eye sockets. Losing my footing, I slid down the wall and hit the floor.

"Chris, what happened? Where are you hit?" I heard Michael say, followed by someone trying to pull me out of my foetal position and force my hands from my face. I growled in pain, through gritted teeth.

"Chris, move your hands, I need to have a look," Michael said. "There's no blood so let me see what it is. Christ, I thought you'd been shot the way you hit the floor."

I loosened up hearing there was no blood, and allowed the right hand to be moved as the stinging pain isolated itself to the left eye.

"Open your eyes!" Michael commanded.

I tried, but my left eye protested, the eyelid squeezed shut. It reminded me of using the peroxide solution used to rinse out a contact lens, once the pain hit, the eyelid shut and you know you need to get it out to stop the pain, but you can't open your eyelid to get at it. Dancing and screaming in pain is all you can do.

"Chris, stand up! You've just got something in your eye, that's all."

"That's all? It stings like a motherfucker!" I yelped.

"You're fine," Michael said. "Calm yourself. We just need to get something to take it out. It's a tiny bit of concrete"

It didn't feel tiny! Alem caught me from my blind side and forced the eye open. Some pressure, a sting and then relief. He had got it.

"What was it?" I enquired, hoping to regain my pride. Alem had used a ten cent Ethiopian Birr to remove a piece of concrete, no bigger than a broken pencil lead.

"And this year's Oscar for best actor goes to…" Michael's sarcasm always brought home how ill-equipped I was to be out here.

Volunteer

"It was the shock of it," I offered as an excuse. "Bastards took a shot at my head."

"Whatever. Let's go." Michael calmly gestured with his head, laughing with the other two as Alem patted my back.

We made it to the town's main street with Michael waving a white piece of cloth at a group of soldiers, who were accompanied by some police officers. Why the hell wasn't I given a white cloth? Did I not need one because I was white? After what had just happened I was not feeling invincible or anything like 'gold dust'.

The advancing troops hugged the walls and took cover behind objects that littered the street. They halted their advance to let us pass as we continued up the street and around the corner. The troops waited until we were out of sight before the gunfire resumed and they continued their assault.

My legs were getting heavy and the sun was taking its toll, I hadn't any water left and my lips had dried up. They had cracked, and bled when I touched them against the back of my hand and they left a bloody print. Right now, my main aim was to concentrate on my running. With the false sense of safety from the increasingly distant sounds of fighting we had slowed our pace, our bodies on a come down from the adrenaline overload. I stared at the ground, and focused on my feet, and I became increasingly aware that I was in danger of tripping, particularly as my left foot kept kicking the back of my right calf. I needed to stop, and rest, I couldn't take much more, but my instinct for survival trumped my failing physical strength.

Michael pointed out 'Hell Hole', and my pace, and spirit, lifted as the finish line came into sight. I had experienced this feeling a hundred times before, over eight years of athletics. This time an audience of erupting explosions, from what had been relatively quiet side-lines, cheered me on. People were already in the large hollow that looked like the mouth of the crater at the top of the mountain in the Cavehill Country Park, back home in Belfast.

Desperate to finally get to cover, my legs gave way and I fell to the ground, arms flailing and I slid forward into the hole, and landed face first, rolling awkwardly over the top of people. Not quite the graceful entrance of a stunt man.

I expected the whole landscape to explode behind me in slow motion. It didn't happen. I rolled onto an injured man, who in fairness didn't make

Volunteer

too much of it. Apologising, I pushed off people and muscled myself into the side wall, trying to keep my head lower than the crater's edge. I didn't want it blown off by a sniper, or for an explosion to disintegrate it to molten ash.

Michael threw his bag into the centre of the crater after watching my glorious entrance, and calmly sat on the edge with his feet dangling in. He threw me a bottle of water, and took out a book and began to read quietly. I drank the water greedily, sucking the air out of the bottle, as if I hadn't tasted a drop of water for days.

"What the fuck are you doing?" I gasped at Michael. "Get your head down! Are you fucking crazy?" I peered over the edge of the crater towards the town that was ghostly quiet now. Nothing outside moved.

"Man, you need to chill the fuck out," Michael said. "The explosions you heard are the Ethiopians hitting the retreating rebel lines. If they hit this spot we're dead, whether you're hiding and shitting yourself, or I'm reading. If that's God's plan, then so fucking be it."

Michael dropped his head back to his book, the silence and flickering eyes told me he was reading. I pushed myself up enough for my whole head to appear above the rim, but there was no sign of fighting on the streets, or noise from nearby explosions. In fact, the sounds were distant, with trickles of smoke snaking their way through the air signalling their impact positions.

I was too scared shitless to read my book, I didn't want to be caught off guard. The day's events replayed over in my head, but at the same time I was bored, a reaction to coming down from an adrenaline rush. This was the first time I had nothing to do, nothing to occupy my time.

"So, why the 'Hell Hole'?" I spoke for the sake of something to say, "Were people killed here?"

"By the size of the crater I'd say there could have been. But that's not why it's called Hell Hole. Do you see the trees shading us?" I looked around.

"There is no shelter, so we're going to roast?" I surmised.

"You've got it in one." Michael smirked. "We're here till the trucks get back, so get the sun cream on, drink plenty of water, cover your head, chill out and shut the fuck up while I'm reading."

Volunteer

The midday sun with no shelter was hell; a cruel heat in a foreign territory, and as a white Northern Irish man, I was going to burn.

After applying a ridiculous layer of sun cream on to my arms and face, I covered my satellite ears. They weren't that big, but I would often joke, when given abuse about the size of them, that 'I could get an extra five hundred channels with these things'. My ears and my nose were always the first to burn, but one thing I could not tolerate was burnt ankles. Thankfully, I was wearing long trousers, socks and boots to keep them covered up.

I lay back, pulled my cap over my face like a cowboy and closed my eyes. The air was still and silent, bar the muffled conversations from some of the locals in the hole with us, not that I paid much attention, my mind was too alert from my heightened senses

The faint hum of a fly was magnified as it worked away, annoying those bold enough to lie on unfazed. The warmth made my skin tingle, as the sun cream soaked in and from the hairs moving as sweat seeped from opened pores.

I drifted into a comfortable state of accidental meditation and I thought of my parents.

They were two wonderful people, but I wasn't sure our relationship was the same as any other parent-child one. But you only ever see the tip of the iceberg with these things and life was always different behind closed doors.

My mum was a short, opinionated woman with a quick temper, who exercised her hand in the belief it was keeping me on the straight and narrow. I'm sure I deserved a slap, but the smallest of things were often blown out of proportion. She was a typical Irish mother, one of the most caring of women who wore her heart on her sleeve and always had a helping hand for those in need.

Mum was the proverbial armadillo; hard on the outside and soft on the inside, she had a thick skin, developed over the years from living with her family at the heart of the troubles. Mum was afraid of no one, but at times the softer side of her nature was evident. She was a protective mother and nanny, loving with a sense of humour. Beyond her hard-faced stare you could see the real emotions of someone who was all heart.

My dad was quite the opposite. Smothered in love and waited on hand and foot by his adoring hard-working parents, he tried to live an easy life, but was often tested by the women in our family,

Volunteer

characterised as being lazy or uncaring. Dad was a stocky man, bald on top with a lifelong, signature moustache. He never got angry and the thought of disappointing him terrified me.

He wasn't just a dad, to me he was a best mate; he was never judgmental and often pushed to hear my scandalous stories, which were exaggerated for him as part of my comic nature. Financially, university had never been an option for him with the pressure of an early marriage. His soft, kind nature was too often abused in our household; if you wanted something you went to dad and he would use his powers of persuasion to influence mum. My sisters and I used him as a human shield to deflect the verbal abuse from mum when we were in trouble.

He was often taken for granted, a man of forgotten dreams and creative regret, a talented man left unchallenged and creatively starved, had he been offered the opportunities as a youth today, he would have excelled effortlessly. I admired, and was inspired, by both of them. I had never had to ask for anything, everything I needed to succeed, in whatever challenge I faced, had been given. I had an unspoken debt to them. Repayment would be making them proud and fulfilling their lost dreams.

Chapter 16: Bloody Reality

The afternoon was much easier than the morning. We walked to the outskirts of town to wander the deserted streets, seeing very little destruction, there were no collapsed or flaming buildings, not even a burned out car, just little pieces of evidence; a small fire, bullet casings, and splashes of blood.

We were looking for the injured, often being called into houses to tend to minor cuts, scratches and shock. It was the first time I was relaxed and comfortable with what I was doing, I was more confident administering first aid than running about dodging bullets. In saying that, I was still nervous and awkward with the language barrier, but was usually rescued by Michael, or one of the two volunteers who had stuck by us.

Regardless, the locals were grateful for the help and, even though I had no idea what people were saying, allowing them to rant was often good

Volunteer

enough for them. They rewarded us with offers of tea or water, which we always made excuses not to take as you never knew the source of the water.

In one particular house, Michael attended to an old woman, in shock from the day's events rather than physically injured. I was kept amused by a toddler, someone fitting my level of communication. It was strange to say, but she didn't look typically Ethiopian, or even part of the family; her skin was lighter and she had a round face, compared to the long faced complexions of everyone else in the room. Not that it was any of my business.

She wore a plain, round-necked, pink T-shirt under a white summer dress that had a scattered flower print over it. Her black hair was pulled tight over her head into a tiny pony tail that was swallowed up by an oversized pink elastic bobble. Everything about her was delicate. She handed me dirty fake flowers, which had been ran over by a car and picked up off the road with her tiny hands, one at the time. She continually talked to herself as toddler's do, laughing occasionally at something she had said to me. I laughed along with her, a betraying look of confusion on my face, not that it mattered to her.

She had a novelty in her house - me - and she was taking full advantage of this opportunity, telling me a story that she didn't have to fight for my attention to tell, or maybe she was having a rant judging by the sudden increase in volume and scolding tone. Often she would cut midway through and look at me, raising her smiling eyes, but not her head, her attention scattered, pointing across the room to random objects.

In my worse Ethiopian pronunciation I asked her name "Simish man naw?" She giggled and ran to hug a young woman who was sitting quietly in the corner room. She patted the little one on the head, and the child ran back to me, but I didn't get an answer.

She pushed a flower into my face and repeated a phrase; I looked around the room for a translation.

"She wants you to smell the flower." Michael laughed. I sniffed the flower and showed over-enthusiastic joy at the odourless plastic stem. Confused at first, she then laughed hysterically. Since arriving in Ethiopia, it was the first time I had heard that kind of laughter and I echoed it.

Volunteer

The exchange was short-lived; an explosion rocked the house and the terrified child grabbed her flowers from my open palm, clutching them to her chest. She held out the one I made her laugh at, I took the blue flower and waved goodbye as she buried her head into the young woman's lap.

We left the small window of happiness and hurried out into the street, running toward the smoke.

As we charged down the main street, a military truck and 4x4 with a 50-caliber machine gun mounted on its back past us and disappeared into the acrid fog. We followed them in to the choking cloud and I pulled my T-shirt up over my nose. Screams rang out, but the stinging smoke rendered me blind and Michael pulled me through to the other side. I overbalanced and fell, confused and irritated; I glared at Michael for an explanation. He signalled an apology and pointed to a smouldering body that was lifeless in the street. I didn't wait around for a closer look, I scrambled to my feet in terror and we continued to run hard.

A young soldier lay unconscious, propped up against a wall and I ran over to attend to him but Michael grabbed at me.

"Not soldiers! They have their own people and their own supplies. If we start helping them we become targets," he explained.

"But he's injured. If we don't help him he'll die," I reasoned.

"Yeah, I get that. But you've got to look at the bigger picture, man. Come on!" I continued down the street, trailed by Michael holding the shoulder strap of my bag. I looked for military medics, and hoped I would see them attend to the soldier, but I never did.

We entered the bomb site and everything unfolded in slow motion. I took in the full extent of the carnage; anything close to the twisted metal that had once been a vehicle, was blackened by smoke, or was in flames. I tried to differentiate between human casualty and structural damage. The volunteers that had arrived before us were trawling the wreckage for casualties.

"Head up the street and get the stretchers out of the trucks!" Michael stood, pointing to the MAA 4x4s. "We'll be lucky if we pull one out of this alive. Hey wake up! It is what it is!" He snapped.

"Ok. Yeah."

Volunteer

I was dazed, confused, trying to analyse the situation. My body was heavy and my head light, the smoke made my breathing slow and forced. I struggled to run to the 4x4, slid the stretchers from the back and awkwardly ran back down the street. Thankfully, there was no wind or it would have looked like a ladder sketch from Laurel and Hardy, flailing all over and tripping over my own feet. I got to Michael and dropped a stretcher beside him. He pointed to a volunteer who was shouting to me.

"Chris kruiwa! Chris Kruiwa" I thought he was just repeating my name in English and Amharic, but 'Kruiwa' meant wheelbarrow. Was this guy calling me a wheelbarrow? I trailed a stretcher over to him and using hand signals he instructed me to put it down and lift on the injured man.

The casualty looked dead. His lower left leg was shredded and I tried to lift him by grabbing his trousers just below the waist pockets. Knowing his wounded limb might touch me, I spread my legs out to create a large enough gap to avoid getting any more blood, or anything else for that matter, on me. The volunteer signalled to lift. There are times in my life were being psychic or having a bird's-eye view of a situation would have been wonderful, and this was one of those times.

Gary McElkerney

I was consumed with not getting blood on me, like some prima donna in an expensive suit. I lifted the casualty up and tried to adjust my footing so as not to stand on the stretcher, but my wide stance had limited the movement of my upper body and I was holding up the weight of the casualty without a proper grip. The fear of dropping him had me off-balance, and the simplest of things was going to make me lose it. And it did.

I heard fizzing, whistling noises and I knew instantly what they were. I flinched from a sudden chill that ran down my spine, followed by what felt like a mist of water from a spray bottle hitting my face at point-blank range. My left foot gave way and I tipped forward falling on top of the casualty, then rolling into the loose gravel. There was an eerie silence between my ears; the distant screams, gunfire and explosions, were suddenly muted. Falling back onto my ass jolted me back to the reality of the situation and in a panic, I grabbed hold of the volunteer to pull myself off the casualty, apologising profusely.

Fear enveloped me, and the air in my lungs became still. I tumbled into the silence of my head and my grip loosened on the volunteer. I pushed away from his body, as Michael checked for some wisp of life in the volunteer. He wouldn't find it.

Volunteer

The man's head had exploded, I was wearing most it, his life was being absorbed by the dust and dried up quickly by the sun.

Bits of him were splattered across my face and I scrubbed furiously, trying to wipe off the top layer of my skin. Michael grabbed at me and I slapped his hand off me and I continued to scrub my face. I wanted to get lost in my own head, away from this, but Michael grabbed my bag straps and T-shirt at the shoulders and screamed in my face.

"Get the fuck up! Move! Come on! Get up!"

He hauled me to my feet and I scrambled for a footing, sliding about. I stumbled as I got the full view, my legs wobbling and I started to vomit. It wasn't seeing the exploded head, it was feeling its residue on my face that had knocked me, but Michael wasn't going to wait or slow the pace. He dragged me along on my knees until I forced myself to my feet.

I fell into the side of the 4x4 and struggled to climb aboard. Michael pushed me up, helping me on like an old dog into the boot of a car and we took off down the road, leaving the ringing of gunfire behind. My body shook; hot tears ran down my face, from emotion, or from retching, or from shock. I buried my head in my dust-covered knees.

I only lifted my head when Michael handed me water, but I couldn't face drinking it.

"It was a tough day, but you came through! You're alive. Be thankful. That doesn't happen every day. That was particularly bad by my standards. Unfortunately, in all this shit we do lose people." He welled up, which was comforting. Sure Michael was a veteran compared to me, but it was reassuring to see that he was still human, that this place hadn't sucked every last emotional response from his body.

"When we get in the shit we get out as quickly as we can." He talked into the distance; he wasn't talking to me or anyone on the back of that 4x4. He was justifying leaving the injured behind - one of our own. "We're not paid to dig in and deal with it, just got to recognise when you're fighting a losing battle."

"What am I supposed to say to people? I mean, how do I figure this shit out in my own head?" I was holding on for his response. I hated the honesty of his answer.

Volunteer

"You don't," he said. "Nobody forgets shit like this. You learn to cope. Just try to hang on to who you are. Lose sight of that, you lose everything. Only way to keep your sanity is to replace days like this with the good things. Out here it's the ones you save, those moments that restore your faith in humanity. Those moments that brought out the best in you."

Like a trigger his words sparked a memory not long lived, the simple gesture of being given a blue plastic flower.

Chapter 17: Face Off

After yesterday's events, we eased into the new day on a lighter note. There was a small farming community that had received some help a few years ago; a charity group had built some houses, to urge them to stay for the stability of a well-made home and good farm land. There had been enough materials and equipment left over to build a school for the local children.

Today, we visited that school and I was the guest of honour, treated to a cheering procession of song and dance as I entered the playground. My spirits lifted as the volunteers from the MAA joined in with the singing and dancing, the usual disheartened, weathered faces replaced with beaming smiles and laughter.

There were two classrooms, fifty odd children crammed in each, of all ages and sizes. The oldest was a boy aged fourteen, but could have passed for eighteen, or even the teacher. It was a similar design to the way we had built the houses in Dessie, the only major difference was that we built the structure with breeze blocks, covered it with cracking cement and a cream painted finish, twisted iron structural rods for windows, a corrugated roof and a red-painted metal door.

The classrooms were a little bigger than the houses we had built, but not suitable for fifty plus children. They had old linear school desks, each with four kids crammed behind, a proper blackboard and the walls had a smooth rendered finish adorned with the usual primary school posters, numbers and random words.

In each class the children welcomed us with songs and reading from English books, and finished up at break time with a quick game of football, with a ball I had bought at a market on the way. What a disorganised game it was; we constructed nets at either end of the 'pitch' by pushing two sticks into the ground, no real teams were formed, just a hundred kids chasing the ball wherever it was kicked or bounced like a pinball.

The volunteers were fighting to establish some uniformity to the game, trying to control the ball and pass it among ourselves. A futile goal when surrounded by excited children within seconds of getting the ball.

Yet again, the fun was short-lived. That dreaded summoning wave from Michael and I strode off, picked up my bag, and headed to the exit, a trail of children hanging onto my arms and wanting up on my shoulders. I had two kids sitting on my feet, arms and legs fully wrapped around both my lower legs, which made walking near impossible. I focused on staying upright. I know kids; I had a three-year old nephew and if you went down you had, unwittingly, volunteered yourself as a human bouncy castle.

The teacher came to my rescue pulling the children from me, restoring my freedom and I jogged to the main entrance with some of the kids tottering alongside me as they waved us goodbye.

There had been a report of a shooting on the outskirts of town by the river, about fifteen minutes' drive from us. We were the closest team, so we headed down the road and after driving for a while to the middle of nowhere, we pulled up beside a long wire fence with tired driftwood posts keeping it in order.

Volunteer

"This is us. We'll only need to bring one of the medical bags," Michael instructed as he walked round to talk to the driver.

I lifted out the bigger of the two bags, not knowing what we were walking into, the radio message had been vague, so we followed Michael's lead and climbed through the wire fence. Even though we were going on a depressing call I have to say I enjoyed the walk. It was a little cloudy with a warm breeze, which was at times nicer than the penetrating sun burning through still air. I had imagined Ethiopia as a dust bowl, a barren desert, especially out here in the far end of nowhere. But it was green with plenty of trees about.

Why couldn't the Hell Hole be here? I would happily spend my time sitting around doing nothing but reading out here.

We arrived at a small clearing occupied by a house, in keeping with the houses my volunteer team was presently building and it was strange to see it all the way out here. It was the home of a part-time police officer. In the smaller towns, most of the men took it in shifts to police the town, but they were farmers first. As we got closer, the disturbing sight of a body hunched over on its knees, hands tied behind its back greeted us. I grabbed Michael's arm.

"It's a trap? I don't see any phone lines. How the hell did they call this in?"

"It's OK. He didn't turn up for work this morning so his colleagues checked in on him, saw this and gave us a call."

"Why didn't they do something, I mean he's one of theirs, why would they just leave him like that?" I was struggling to get my head round this. It was too convenient. Michael instructed the other two team members to go into the house and speak to the family.

"Listen, these guys volunteer as police for the extra income. It's a part-time job to them. Out here farming is the way of life. They maintain law and order as a visual presence only, and that's it. They aren't medics. If that was the case we'd be out of a job." He grinned and shrugged.

As we approached the body a chilling scream came from inside the house. A woman ran towards us. I stepped back, getting ready to run if I had to. She shook her arms at us in a flapping movement to get back, and Michael put his hand in front of my chest as I tried to stop her going near, to hide her from the horror.

She had already seen the body from the house, and dropped in front of him, placing her hands delicately on his head. She dropped her head to his and wailed out her loss. Moments of whispering were followed by silence. Her clothes were torn and falling from her body, revealing her bruised, cut skin. It was evident that she had recently taken a harsh beating.

A second, older woman emerged from the house sobbing quietly, a blanket covering her battered body. My blood ran cold and I froze. I had a fair idea what had happened here. A mix of anger and shock was building inside me, churning in to an overwhelming sadness.

Michael told me that the rebels had turned up to the house and dragged the two women and the man outside, savagely beating all three and then forced the women to watch as they beat the man until he begged for death as a trade for the women's lives. He had been tied up and shot numerous times, used as a target for their amusement. Then the women, one the wife of the policeman the other his mother, were dragged back into the house and beaten some more while the rebels raped them in turn. I brought my hands to my head and trailed them down my face, pulling at the skin and sank to a squat position.

If there is one thing I can't have and was brought up by my mum to hate, it is violence of any form against women or children. Even films that show it I find hard to watch. It was the first time I had felt this sort of rage and I was convinced that if we had got here in time to catch the bastards, I would have killed them all. To add to the misery, the rebels had found a baby boy, only a year old, who had been hidden in the house by his mother, and they had taken him.

"What will they do with him?" I asked. "Keep him and train him as a soldier?" I dreaded the answer, and I was willing to hunt them down to return the baby to his mother.

"Who knows? Could have left him in a forest for animals to get him? My best guess is they dumped him in the river. He's too young to take on and look after"-Michael tapped my back-"Right let's go. Family wishes to sort him out in their own time so we'll leave some medical supplies for the women and respect their wishes."

Volunteer

"Shouldn't we go and look for the baby? They can't have got far."

I was desperate to try to salvage something from this; we couldn't bring the husband back, but if we were able to return the child it would make things better.

"It's a nice thought man, but we could search all week and not find that kid. They don't take a kid for us to play 'hide and go seek' with. Kid is already dead. Losing battles man. It's tough I know, especially with a baby involved, but it is what it is. Come on."

I knew he was right and that was the hard part to face up to, having the will power to do something that would result in nothing.

It's hard enough at funerals to come up with the right words, and I had nothing to offer these women, my words were worthless. I felt useless, overcome with guilt, as if I bore some responsibility for this tragedy. I came here to help people, but I wasn't comforting people, offering assistance or making things better. So, how was I helping?

We walked in silence, the other guys feeling as helpless as me. I stared at my feet until Michael diverted my attention.

153

"Whoa! Whoa!"

He motioned for us to slow our pace. Standing at the tree line, with his rifle pointed at us was a child no more than twelve years of age, and by Michael's reaction, a rebel. The boy stood unfazed by our presence, wearing a pair of army regulation camouflage trousers with the bottoms cut off below the knee and only sandals on his feet. He also wore a navy vest that would have been big on me, never mind him. It hung off his stick-thin frame, probably came free with his oversized rifle. He leaned back, arching his spine to brace himself against the weight of the gun. I approached with my hands out showing him I was unarmed.

"What the fuck are you doing?" Michael whispered, so as not to panic the child.

"He's not going to shoot me. Ask him if he knows about the shooting down the road." I had fixed my gaze on him, anger forcing the air out through my nose, but I tried to appear calm so I didn't alarm him.

"Fuck it man. We know he does."

"Just ask him," I persisted.

Volunteer

Michael asked the question. The boy was getting edgy and stepped forward pointing the gun at me as he answered.

"What did he say?" I asked. Michael hesitated.

"That he was shooting a dog."

"There were no dogs." I said. Confused, I glanced at Michael.

"He means the cop."

The cocky bastard slow-cocked the rifle with a smirk.

"Tell him to give me the weapon," I ordered.

"Dude he isn't going to give you the rifle. Come on, let's just fucking go," Michael laughed, nervously, but I was fixated on getting this gun.

"Tell him!" I refused to take my eyes off the kid as I strategically moved my hands closer together almost begging for him not to shoot. His answer, translated by Michael, was 'White shit, go fuck yourself'.

"Tell him that we don't want any trouble. We are aid workers and we don't want to get hurt."

As Michael spoke to the two other terrified aid workers to assist with translation, the boy turned towards them and so did the gun. This was exactly what I had waited for. I grabbed the rifle, forcing the barrel skywards, and gripped the kid by the throat. The rifle went off and I jumped, but tightened my hold around his throat. I had used this technique in school as an effective defence against bullies, grabbing the trachea and squeezing it between my thumb and the knuckle on my index finger.

"Drop it you wee bastard or I'll fucking kill you!" I growled through my teeth. He grabbed at my hand, with his left hand as he wriggled, but refused to let go of the rifle. So I tightened my grip. Close to the point of passing out, he finally let go and I threw him back.

Crashing to the ground, he fought for breath, coughing violently, but quickly got to his feet and came at me. Surprising us both, I cocked the rifle and lifted it in one smooth action, taking aim at his head. He stopped dead in his tracks.

"Whoa! Whoa!"

Panic rose in Michael's voice, trying to regain control of the situation.

"Back the fuck off!"

Volunteer

Understanding the tone, if not the words the young rebel retreated. The rifle was heavy. How on earth had this child carried it around or shot anything with it? It wasn't until he was out of view that I lowered the gun, relieved to see him gone and surprised that my tactics had worked.

I had been told there was nothing scarier than a child with a gun and they weren't wrong. That little shit would have punctured me with bullets and not thought twice about it. They didn't know any better, so I sure as fuck wasn't going to turn my back to him and walk on. I was getting the impression these fuckers didn't need a reason to kill you. White or not I wasn't taking the chance.

"What the fuck was that?" Michael asked, confused by my actions, as was I to be honest, still shaking with adrenaline. How fucking cool was that?

"I got his gun"-I shrugged, as if that justified my actions-"let's see him kill or rape someone else without it. Even better, let's see him defend himself."

That was all talk; I didn't want to see the child get hurt or killed.

In part, I believed I had done the right thing, but I should have dealt with it better. With the residual anger from what we had seen today still pumping through me, I thought that if the kid had gone for me I might have shot him in the face.

Was I capable of killing? Yesterday I couldn't handle seeing someone shot in front of me. How would I have been able to handle the guilt of killing a child, wiping someone's existence from this earth?

"Shit like that has consequences man. Just hope to fuck it isn't on us." Michael was annoyed, but I didn't care; I was buzzing. I held that rifle and walked with the authority of a military patrol. Fuck consequences; I had a rifle and if they wanted to come for me I was ready, or so my ego told me.

When we passed a group of rebel men gesturing with abusive signals from the opposite side of the river, I stared them down. If they had come at me I imagined I would fire off a few shots to delay them so I could leg it up the hill, probably throwing the rifle somewhere so it wouldn't weigh me down. There was also no chance I was going to go across and get their guns off them. They would have outnumbered me, nothing to do with the fact I didn't have the guts.

Volunteer

With no more calls to make we headed back to the clinic to rest up. Thankfully, we didn't have far to go because the trip back was awkward. Michael wouldn't look at me, never mind talk to me and he took out a book and pretended to read. The truck bounced and vibrated so much on the dirt roads you were lucky if you could focus to read a road sign never mind a novel. I stared down at the rifle I was holding in place with my feet. My trophy.

As we pulled into the clinic courtyard, Odette was sitting on the steps sunbathing without her headscarf on, and the straps of her top hung loosely around her arms to avoid a thin white tan line. We pulled into a free parking space beside the other MAA 4x4s and Michael threw his book into his bag and swung his legs over the side. I picked up the rifle and Odette walked over.

"Where did you get that?" I froze struggling to come up with a better answer than 'I found it'.

Michael came to sink me. "Rambo here took down a LF rebel and lifted his rifle; a child no less." He smiled, shouldering his bag. "Leave that where it is." He instructed, striding towards the clinic.

Odette sighed, not with disappointment, but with acceptance. She wasn't surprised. I replied how I knew best, with humour.

"I was worried he'd hurt himself."

"I'm sure." She tapped me gently.

Entering the clinic, Michael was waiting and threw me a towel. "We're going to grab showers here and head to where I'm staying for a drink in about half an hour." Knowing Odette was just outside he shouted to her as he started for the showers. "Odette, I expect you to join us. You're hardly run off your feet here."

"Oh showers together and then drinks. All on the first date?" I joked, as Michael walked backwards.

"I'm only promising drinks," he laughed. "Plus technically, this would be, what the third date? And anyway, you know what they say, once you go black?" We laughed and I walked down the corridor to my room to drop off my bag. Sensing Odette had entered, I turned.

"Shall I meet you here in half an hour?"

"Yes." She smiled and with a nod I raced up the stairs like an excited child. This was the first time we had properly spoken and now we were going for drinks together. Thank you, Michael.

Volunteer

I wouldn't have had the balls to ask her, didn't even know there was a bar here. Not that I had any prospects with Odette, this girl was out of my league and my nerves would get the better of me anyway. So, I would play the funny guy, placing myself firmly in friend zone as usual. What would be the point anyway? I was only going to be here another week or so, and then be unlikely to ever see her again. The most I hoped for was an email address. Sure, she was probably with Michael anyway.

Chapter 18: Rest and Recuperation

We walked towards town, about fifteen minutes from the clinic, and stopped in front of an odd-looking structure. It reminded me of something out of a documentary on the Iron Age. A round building with clay walls, which in places revealed its manmade tree formation, and supported a thatched roof of long, thin twigs.

We walked through the open door and into what transpired to be the local bar, and I have to say I was pleasantly surprised. I expected the place to be dark and dingy inside, but instead, it was open on either side with a perimeter of light bulbs around its radius and along the cross-beams.

"Are you wearing make-up?" Michael asked.

"No," I smirked.

"No!" Odette blushed. "Well, maybe." She lowered her voice as we approached the bar.

Volunteer

"I've never seen her with make-up on." Michael pointed out. I hadn't really noticed the make-up; as far as the whole package went she looked different. She wore a long black skirt with an orange vest top and a short black cardigan. Her hair was tied in a ponytail, completely different from her clinic style. I caught her glaring at Michael and jumped in to break the awkwardness.

"She looks lovely, at least she made the effort." Neither of us had. I barely dared to hope that she had made the effort for me.

"Well, yeah, it's a night out, and how often do we get those?" Michael agreed, restoring the relaxed mood.

There were beers on draft and rows of shelves on the back wall filled with spirits and wine, bottles of different sizes and shapes, brands I had never heard of.

"What are you having?" Michael asked. My eyes darted across the bar to the draft beers and then the shelves searching for Castel, the only beer I knew and was safe with.

"I would recommend St. George's, it's a beer made in Addis," the barman said, through Michael's translation, "bit strong on taste, but nice."

"Castel?" I asked

"You want a half litre of it or a bottle?" Michael asked.

"Half a litre, please." I took my wallet out, confused by the measurement. What was wrong with a pint?

"I got this man, you get the next round. Hey Odette! What you having to drink?"

Odette had sat down at one of the rows of fixed picnic style tables.

"Yeah I'll have a half litre of Castel too actually. Nice evening for it." She surprised me, with a French name I was expecting her to order red wine, or something more sophisticated.

"You take those down to the table." Michael handed me the two glasses of Castel and I carried them over to Odette. I sat opposite her and Michael jumped down beside her.

"What are you drinking?" I asked him.

"Fanta Orange."

"No alcohol?" I found his choice strange, since drinks were his suggestion

Volunteer

"I don't drink man, never have. It's not a Christian thing before you ask, just don't really need it."

"That's cool. I'm Northern Irish, that's my excuse." True, I liked a drink, but I didn't live up to the hype of the 'Irish Curse'. I was guilty of jumping onto the ego bandwagon professing myself to be a big drinker to impress. Yes I had been known to drink my own body weight on a night out, but it didn't happen often, and most times I found myself going out and staying sober. Tonight, however, I was on my holiday, so it couldn't hurt.

"Oh shit," Michael whispered, quietly, into his drink.

"What?" I leaned towards him.

"That guy who just walked in," Michael kept his voice low, "nice enough, just in your face. Quite full on."

Pot. Kettle. Black. You would never catch an American being in your face, or full on.

"Ah, Michael! My friend, how are you tonight?" The man called out as he pointed in our direction. He reminded me of Amare only stockier, his beard thinly trimmed, a fashion accessory on his face like a rapper's, which looked out of place around here. He wore a dark brown pair of washed out jeans and a pale blue shirt that was a size too big for him. He landed a big hand on Michael's shoulder as he sat down.

"Jamal, I'm good as always man, and you?" Michael faked an expression of interest.

"Same as always, busy." He gestured with an upwards nod of his head, pouting his lips in 'duck face' pose. "Who are your friends?"

"You know Odette, from the clinic," Michael said.

"Odette? Are you wearing make-up?" Jamal laughed. Odette flashed a tight smile, not amused that, for the second time, it was highlighted. "I didn't recognise you."

"And this is Chris, just arrived this week to give me and the clean-up crew a hand." Michael nodded at me.

"You American too?"

"No, I'm Northern Irish."

"Same as Irish? You boys can drink, no?" With a booming laugh he extended his hand and I

Volunteer

took it with one firm shake. "Welcome to Ethiopia my friend."

I didn't really see a problem with Jamal, he appeared harmless enough, just a little loud and excitable, perhaps, but he meant well.

"Michael. Come to the bar. I buy you another and we catch up." Jamal got up and Michael followed him, rolling his eyes.

"Talk to you in a bit," he said reluctantly to us, leaving Odette and me at the table in silence. I sat for a bit sneaking glances at Odette, and then trying to look anywhere and everywhere else, but at her.

"So, what's your story? What brought you here?" I blurted out to break the silence. It occurred to me that I'd met her a week ago, but didn't actually know anything about her.

"I'm training to be a nurse," she said. "And decided to take a gap year and work here for a while. I started in Addis, but wanted something more challenging. You know?"

"Not half. It's the reason I'm here." She looked confused.

"Things are bad at home, so you packed up and came all the way here?" she asked, "Are you travelling around the world?" I saw her eyes light up in anticipation of an exciting story, a shame to extinguish them.

"No, things are fine at home. I decided to come here and build houses instead of going away on holiday. I got bored in Dessie. Travelled up here to torture you guys for a while. How long have you got left?"

"I have another few months, up to October. Then back home," Odette said. "I live in Southampton, but I go to University in London."

"London? Sorry, I thought you were from France?" I was confused and embarrassed.

"I am. Moved to Southampton when I was eleven but the accent has stuck."

"Well, everyone finds an accent attractive." The sentence literally fell out of my mouth and my face reflected my embarrassment.

"Yes we do," Odette said. She saved me, but embarrassed herself in the rescue.

Volunteer

I went to get more drinks and casually left Michael's Fanta at his hand, so as not to disturb him. He was still stuck in a deep conversation with Jamal. I brought two more Castels back to the table.

"So, what about the doctor? What's his story?" I asked.

"Emmanuel? His story is, well, lovely and sad. But of course I'm French and a romantic, so I would think that." As she spoke, her eyes lowered to her drink "The doctor has two children but was divorced for many years. Finally, he met a woman he had loved when he was a young man - she had married someone else because, at that time, he was too focused on his studies. He bumped into her in the hospital and they took up where they had left off, and their loved blossomed."

She took a drink and paused for a moment to look at me. I tried to keep my face emotionless, I had recently become single; love stories were not exactly up there with my favourites at the moment.

"Is that it?"

"No. They were engaged within no time, but the reason she was in hospital when they met, was that she was being tested for something - he never said what – but she had a series of tests to pinpoint what was wrong. Despite treatment, she got progressively worse and he stayed with her the entire time, helping or just sitting with her for company. She tried to break off the engagement, convinced she wasn't going to make it, but he refused. Finally, the date of their wedding came, but she couldn't make it to the ceremony."

"Did she die?" Stirrings of empathy as the tale moved from a love story to one of mourning.

Odette took another drink. I had finished my pint, absorbed in the story.

"No, be patient and listen," Odette scolded, playfully slapping my hand. "She was in a coma for two weeks and slowly, over a few months, she came back to full health. But no sooner had they rebooked the wedding, she was back in the hospital."

Jesus Christ, was she making this up - who goes into a coma and then recovers only to get sick again?

"She got worse a lot faster this time, and again tried to break off the engagement. Instead, the doctor organised to marry her in the hospital there and then. Which they did. Within days she was back in a coma, and for the rest of their honeymoon he sat at her side. Eventually, her body gave in and she

Volunteer

died. The doctor took the money he had saved for the wedding, moved out here, built the clinic and has been here ever since."

"What did she die of?"

"He never said."

I felt like I was sitting at a wake, one of those awkward moments when you the need to say something to break the deafening silence. It explained who the woman was in the picture in his office.

"What about you?" I broke the silence awkwardly. "Boyfriend? Michael?" What better way to follow up that story than with more relationship talk?

"Michael? Oh he's lovely, but not really my type. Too loud and in your face. He's more like an older brother. I'm single. With nursing and travelling it doesn't give me enough time for a boyfriend. So, I'm happy to do without the pressures of a relationship. There's no rush. And you?"

I hadn't expected the question to turn back on me. While I was struggling to come up with a response, Michael returned.

"What you guys talking about?" Michael eyed us with suspicion as he dropped down beside me. "Looks serious."

"I'm single too. Recently broken up," I confessed quickly.

"Seriously? I leave you guys for ten minutes and you're flirting? You need some time alone?" We laughed nervously and Odette stood up.

"Same again?" She asked. We nodded an answer and she headed for the bar.

"My Irish friend, you like our bar?" Jamal asked, following Michael back to our table. I scanned the bar as if taking it in before answering.

"Yeah it's a nice bar, just what you want after a hard day."

"So, you are on the frontline with Michael? How you finding it?" Jamal asked.

"Yeah, it's been tough. Not what I expected, but hanging in there one day at a time," I said. Then out of nowhere I was hit with a question that chilled me.

"Do you think you could kill someone, if you had to?" Jamal asked, eyeing me. I was stunned.

Volunteer

I mean, what the fuck? This guy didn't even know me, what sort of question was that to ask?

"What do you mean?" I asked, hoping he was joking.

"Do you think that you have the ability to kill someone?" He asked again, in all seriousness

I wanted someone to interrupt, but the table went quiet, waiting for my answer. I hadn't even noticed Odette come back, but she sat looking at me expectantly, too.

"I guess if my life depended on it, or someone was trying to kill me, it's a possibility," I hedged, "but I'd try to maybe hurt or maim them instead, I guess. Doubt I'd just kill them." I rolled over the words, confused by where this was going, and my face showed it.

"Of course you can kill someone, everyone has the ability," Jamal grinned. "You are an animal. The only difference is animals kill to live. Humans kill because we can, for no reason at all."

"What's that got to do with me drinking in a bar?" I asked defensively. I felt cornered and uncomfortable.

"Nothing. Just be prepared is all. You hear stories from the frontline. Stay safe my friend!" And with that Jamal left. I sat motionless for a second, before turning to Michael.

"What the fuck was that?" I was genuinely annoyed and confused.

"Nothing man, he's like that," Michael said, taking a drink of his Fanta. "Ignore him. He's a fucking delivery driver, knows nothing at all about the frontline. He talks the big talk, but you won't find him anywhere near trouble." We sat in silence. "Let's finish our drinks and head back to the clinic, early start tomorrow."

We agreed and rushed down the drinks just to get out of the bar before Jamal came to enlighten us with more of his wisdom.

Chapter 19: Consequence or Coincidence

The next morning, after the usual breakfast of toast and tea, I found myself in Emmanuel's office, initially summoned by Odette. He had been looking for me and I was convinced I was in trouble for the rifle incident. It was a long walk to the office the whole time trying to create a good enough reason to excuse my actions, when the truth of the matter was I couldn't even explain it. I knocked on the office door and entered, Emmanuel was working at his desk.

"You were looking for me?" I hung by the doorway.

"Come in, come in. Please take a seat." He gestured, with his hand, but there were no chairs. I noticed a stool sitting to the right of his desk, but it wasn't the sturdiest. I left the office, to Emmanuel's confusion and returned with one of the cheap plastic chairs with the slanted metal legs from the hallway. It hit the floor noisily as I swung it in front of the desk. I screwed up my face in embarrassment and quietly sat down, preparing myself for the interrogation.

"Why didn't you take that chair?" He pointed past me to the back of the office where there was a perfectly presented red upholstered soft chair, the type you get in hotel seminar rooms.

"This is fine," I said. I looked at the picture of the woman on his desk and I wanted to ask him who she was, if it was the woman from Odette's story. More so I was curious to know what the hell she had died of.

"I just wanted to inform you that I have been in touch with Colin and Roisin. Just to let them know that you're with us at the clinic, that everything is fine, and that your help here has been much appreciated. Which of course it is. I know it's difficult at times, but you seem to be coping with everything quite well."

It was a relief to hear that not only was this not about the rifle incident, but that I wouldn't be heading back to explain myself either. As for the

Volunteer

difficult times, I thought I was pretty useless, I wasn't coping at all.

Just then Michael burst into the office. "We've got a call and we need to move right now!"

"What? Right! OK!" I had no idea what was going on. Was Michael helping me out with the old 'I'm on an awkward date emergency telephone call' or was it something serious?

"We're done," Emmanuel dismissed me with a wave of his hand. "Go quickly!"

"Thanks!" I trailed the chair across the floor and flung it against the wall outside the office, sprinting down the hall after Michael.

"I'll just grab my bag!" I shouted, running up the stairs,

"You won't need it. Come on, now!" He shouted from the door waiting for me; this was serious.

"Why? Where are we going?"

"Where we were yesterday."

We rushed towards the 4x4s ignoring Odette. I was nervous, Michael was never this alarmed.

"Why would they attack the family again? Did we miss something?" All this panic and haste had me breathless.

"No! They hit the fucking school!" Slapping the side of the 4x4, Michael screamed at the driver. "God damn it! Let's go already!"

We raced along the road, it was the longest journey. Yesterday it was a beautiful drive back to the clinic, but today, though the weather may have been better, there was no time for kicking back and taking it in. Every time we came up behind another vehicle I screamed at it to move out of our way. Not that they heard me, with the wind snatching away my pleas.

With every hill I hoped we had arrived. I was ready to go, ready to bounce off the 4x4 and get stuck in. This was different, I hadn't gained in confidence or got used to things, but I had made a connection with this school. I was their guest of honour, but above all else these were children.

We pulled up to the entrance. The trees that lined the road had covered the view of the school, but we heard the gunfire echoing from across the hill, opposite the school. We jumped off the 4x4 and Michael and I were immediately surrounded by

Volunteer

screaming parents and siblings. I tried desperately to break through the crowd as they pulled at my clothes. I really didn't have the patience to deal with them right now; my main concern was to see the damage. Michael broke free and shouted at one of the volunteers who ran towards the entrance of the school screaming wildly.

What the fuck was going on? I watched as a crowd of men tried to grab hold of Michael, who easily broke through them to the entrance. The gunfire suddenly picked up and I heard Michael scream. What was I going to do if he was shot? What was he thinking? He was never this careless! Too much was happening, I was losing control. There was no guidance, no organisation. This was fucking chaos.

As I made it to the entrance, I was relieved to see Michael alive and well. However, he was trailing a volunteer along the ground; it was Alem, holding his stomach with bloodied hands, sobbing through the pain and shock. I ran back to the truck to grab the medical packs, this time I had zero patience for wailing people getting in my way.

"Move! Move!" I screamed. I was no longer fucking around and happy to push people out of my way. The driver handed me two bags and I turned back towards the entrance, this time the crowd shifted out of my way, I ran to Michael and dropped the bags beside him, crouching down.

"You're going to be alright Alem, just hang tight mate," I offered as words of comfort, which were useless as he didn't speak any English.

"What the fuck was he doing?" I asked.

"Fuck man I don't know. He has a kid, or a relative, or something in the school, so he went to get them." Michael was working with another volunteer on stopping the bleeding.

I looked at Alem's path to the school and noticed the pile of bodies at the entrance of each classroom.

"They've got the kids pinned inside the classrooms," Michael said. "As soon as the parents try to make a run for it they are gunned down."

I walked to the edge of the entrance, just staying under cover, and spotted a number of bodies strewn about the playground. I was fixated on the football, a gift I had given the children just yesterday, now covered in blood. Coincidence or consequence? Would they have been outside if I

Volunteer

hadn't given them the ball? A simple gift had turned into a death sentence.

"What are we going to do?" I asked.

Michael applied pressure to a large rolled up mess of bandages that covered Alem's stomach.

"I don't know. Wait it out? We can't get them to make a run for it, would be like shooting fish in a fucking barrel." He rubbed his face with the back of his forearm. "I don't fucking know."

This alarmed me; for the first time Michael was genuinely lost, and mentally exhausted. Yet it suddenly all became clear. This was on me. I knew what I had to do. I felt exactly as I did on the first day clinging to that 4x4, but I couldn't back out of this. I took off my cap and sunglasses and threw them beside one of the bags on the ground.

"Whatever you are thinking, forget it," Michael said, keeping his eyes on Alem, who was fading into a blood drained sleep. "We need to get him back to the clinic."

I stared at the ground, deep in thought; I was finished with this shit. All of us sitting around, helpless, but making excuses to do nothing.

"I can do this. In case you forgot, I'm white, I'm gold dust. Just get ready to take the kids off me."

"And what if I was wrong about that?" Michael asked.

"Then I will be really pissed at you." I tried to hide my fear, but I was giving it away clicking my fingers on both hands. I had a strong image of me getting cut down, just like Alem and ending up lying beside him, in my own blood. "Luckily for you though, I'll be dead and they will have started up a shit storm."

The glorious death I had once imagined, I really didn't want it, but I had no choice. I cautiously walked to the entrance with my hands out in front of me in plain view. I've no idea why. I mean, this wasn't a negotiation and I wasn't surrendering. I was shaking, half expecting to get ripped to pieces in a swarm of bullets. Had they fired off a few shots I'm pretty sure I would have pissed myself at the noise.

Just as Michael said it would, the shooting stopped. I picked up the pace, remembering to breathe, and jogged to the first classroom. I ignored the bodies strewn across the field and took the quickest route to get out of view.

Volunteer

The kids greeted me with fearful screams. Obviously, they weren't expecting someone to come for them, the oldest kid in the class approached me, the fourteen year old, who had taken control. Their teacher lay in a puddle of blood just outside the classroom, but the children, who had hidden on the floor, slowly surrounded me. They were crying with fear, but filled with relief that I had come. I pushed my way further into the room to keep them from the entrance so they couldn't be picked off.

"Tell them to stay down and I'll come and get them. But they need to stay in here no matter what. Tell them it's OK. You understand?" I addressed the oldest kid, speaking slowly with more diction, using sign language for clarity.

"Everyone stays in here. I promise I will come and get you. Do not leave this room, no matter what. OK?"

He nodded and shouted the orders. Some of the smallest ones whimpered. I tried to leave the class, carefully pulling away from the vice like grips of the terrified youngest children who were desperate to go with me. I wanted to pick them all up, to hug each one of them, but instead, I tried to console them with a pat on the head, or a stroke of the cheek, wiping away tear tracks with my thumb, telling them it was okay. It was gut wrenching, but this was not the time for emotion.

Again, I put my hands up as I ran to the next classroom, unsure if I was still being watched. The teacher was still present and on the floor, so I issued out the same instructions to a much calmer response and offered two thumbs up and a smile. Then I ran back to the first class to the sound of random gunfire. I guess that kind of answered the question of whether I was still being watched. I dived to the ground immediately, but the sound of muffled screams forced me back to my feet. I sprinted through the door of the first classroom and once again I was completely swamped by tearful children, and desperate little hands grabbing at my clothes. How the hell was I going to do this?

"What's your name?" I asked the oldest kid. "Ah, simish man naw?"

"Kaleb."

"Kaleb? Your name is Kaleb?"

"Yes," he nodded, urgently.

"You speak English?"

"Yes I understand, but not a lot."

Volunteer

"That's grand. I need you to organise them. Youngest children first."

"In a line?"

"Yeah roughly, doesn't have to be exact."

Kaleb waited for a word or a phrase he recognised. How could I make this fucking easier? Fuck it. I didn't have time to give out an English lesson. I lift the first kid, a girl who was probably nine or ten, who was injured. Kaleb had started queuing up children against the wall.

I pointed to the first child in the queue, a tiny girl, and crouched down patting my back. She climbed on and I pushed her up with one arm behind my back, trying not to lose my balance, while also holding the injured girl in my arms. I struggled to stand up, her tiny arms wrapping tightly around my neck.

The next child, a little boy who must have been only four or five, had cried his eyes out the entire time I was there. I had him hold onto my trouser pocket, to keep him close to me so he wouldn't get picked off by the gunmen. With that came the moment of truth as we left the sanctity of the classroom.

I walked with baby steps. Maintaining my composure and keeping the children calm. If they wanted to kill the kids they would have to hit me and we couldn't be having that. I hurried towards Michael, finding it hard to judge my speed with a child being pulled along holding my pocket, struggling to keep on his feet; his tear-filled eyes blurred his vision. All three children, realising they were close to freedom and away from danger, cried out for their relatives. Michael and a volunteer grabbed the kids from me once in the safe cover of the trees, and I immediately turned and ran back to the classroom.

I entered the classroom to more eager hands in the air, the next few in the queue begging to be picked up. Being more adventurous and having established that the LF were not going to take a risk, I grabbed the first five kids in the queue and made my way back out to the waiting party. I had one on my back, one in my arms, one holding my right pocket, one holding my left, and another holding my right hand. It was taking too long, but it was the only solution I had.

Back and forth I went, begging hands and tearful wet faces pleaded to be lifted to safety, and relatives imploring me to save their children. The class had calmed down a bit and was more

Volunteer

organised with Kaleb standing in the middle of the room talking softly to his much younger classmates. I gave him an encouraging 'thumbs up' each time, I returned to keep up the good work as I took out four and five kids at a time.

I had done about six runs when a gunman took a shot at the second classroom as someone looked out at our progress. As I turned to tell them to stay in the classroom, one of the kids let go of my pocket and made a run for the pleading crowd. I charged after him trailing one of the kids by the arm, even if I could just get close to him it might deter them from shooting. Luckily, we all made it to the safe cover of the tree and I dropped the other three kids off with Michael.

"You need to tell the relatives to shut the fuck up, or get them out of sight!" It was tiredness speaking out. The kids didn't weigh much, but it was tiring nevertheless, and emotions ran high. The sun was beating down and I hadn't stopped to suck in air.

"They're upset. Me telling them to shut up will not help," Michael snapped back. Then added more calmly, "it's hard enough to keep them from making a run for the school. You're doing fine. Keep it up."

He was right, of course, and I had amazed myself, stepping up to the challenge. I had finally proved something to myself. This was my moment. Just as I started my heroes walk towards the school for my next pick up, Michael let out an explosive scream.

"Get down!"

A familiar noise screamed through the still air. It echoed around the area and for a moment I thought this was it. At least I'd be going out with a bang.

But it wasn't me they aimed for.

The roof and the side walls of the school exploded. My body shuddered with the flash, the delayed sound of the explosion slowed down my reactions, as if my brain needed to be reset. The sound wave passed through us and I flinched putting my arm up and turning from the heat of the tumbling ball of flames. I stumbled over my feet, losing my bearings. My mind had gone blank. Was I even breathing? What the fuck just happened? I staggered forward, concentrating on making my lungs work, both arms raised, hands on the sides of my head. I let out a long scream.

"Fuck!"

Volunteer

I felt Michael grab my left arm and I tried to pull away from him, my eyes fixed on the hypnotic lick of the flames that escaped from the remaining walls. I kept screaming, to block out the emotional pain that threatened to overcome me. Michael pulled at me again and I kept fighting him. My brain shut down, cancelling any rational response as it focused on imprinting the unfolding event on my memory. He got in front of me and I fought to walk past him, drawn to the school like an insect to a light. Our arms locked in a tangled hold on each other. He grabbed the sides of my face, trying to break my line of sight, forcing my eyes to focus with his.

"They're gone! They're dead!" His voice quivered. "We tried!" He shook my head, rattling my brain for a response. "They're dead. You tried."

"Someone will have survived. We…we can save them." I was desperate to believe that, the blast couldn't have killed all of them.

"No, it's over," he said.

"No! No, it's not," I said, "I know I can find someone. I can save *someone*. I promised them! I promised them I would get them out."

I wasn't done, I was sure there were more children to save, but at that moment a tiny, flaming body fell through the door of the first classroom. It sucked the air from my lungs. My arms dropped to my side. My eyes filled. I could do nothing. Tears finally broke through Michael's red-eyed stare and ran in tracks down his dusty skin.

He ran to help the volunteers keep the relatives back, and attend to people who had fainted, or were possessed with grief. In contrast, I was brain-dead, motionless. Finally, I dragged my useless body away from the school towards the truck and slid down the side of it. I couldn't even sit upright, I was a dead weight, my breath forced, staring at the school.

I had often seen in movies how things suddenly go quiet; all picture, with muffled sounds in slow motion, as the camera captures the emotional drama. It was close, but not strictly accurate. The sound was possibly fainter, but my tears blurred the picture even though I couldn't cry. The shock was paralysing, my mind too overloaded to take in the scene.

I can't remember how long I sat there. Gravity cleared my eyes, pushing tears down my face and partially restored my vision.

Volunteer

Eventually, I reached up to the side of the 4x4 and pulled myself to my feet, taking a minute or so to regain my composure. Then, reaching into the back of the truck, I lifted the rifle. I walked towards the entrance to the school with a purpose; fuck this, I'd had enough of tiptoeing round these fuckers. Cowering behind our morals, waiting for them to leave evidence of their bullshit cause while we came in behind and cleaned up their mess.

Despite all the commotion and panic, Michael heard the bolt-action of the rifle and ran at me from the side, grabbed at the rifle with both hands and pulled it from me. Throwing it to one side, he pushed me back.

"What the fuck are you doing?" He growled at me, voice lowered so no one else heard. I shrugged. I had no justification for what I was doing. I avoided his eyes.

"That doesn't help! How the fuck is that productive? So, you're going to kill them in revenge for this?" He pointed towards the inconsolable crowd.

"They don't want that! It doesn't matter who does the killing, justified or not, it is still wrong."

Gary McElkerney

I knew what I wanted to do, but had no idea of how to go about it. Right now, I wasn't a soldier, a medic, or a self-proclaimed hero in my own head. I was nothing; a useless wreck in the face of this. I stared down to one of the kids I'd just rescued, she was wrapped around my leg with her arms and legs, quite possibly as she had done the day before at the football game, too young to understand the nature of the situation, she offered a smile. I had nothing to give.

Chapter 20: Breakdown

Eventually the fires died down, as did the tortured wails of the parents, that at first were gut wrenching to listen to, then became increasingly annoying. I imagined grabbing some of them by the shoulders and shaking them, slapping them even. Eventually, I just blanked them out.

I had taken my seat back by the side of the 4x4 and I watched a team of makeshift fire fighters douse the flames with a train of 'pass the bucket' with water from barrels on the trucks. I would like to say I hadn't the energy to help. The truth of it was, I didn't give a fuck. What difference did it make? Where was the LF now? Plenty of people to gun down here, but then killing adults didn't have the same impact.

After a short while, the greyish white smoke began to dissipate, Michael ventured my way. "Get up! Let's finish this."

"Finish this?" I wasn't sure if this was his emotional defence mechanism, or just a job to him, but how would we 'finish this', unless he meant we were going to hunt the bastards down.

"Finish what?" I asked.

"We need to take the bodies out of the school and lay them out on the playing field for the families."

"You fucking what?" Was he taking the piss? So, finish the job I had started, go in there and lift three or four kids, dead ones this time, and throw them on the grass, line them up to see what the percentage of success was?

"We need to do this for the families."

"What because I fucked up? Because I didn't get them out quick enough?" I pulled myself to my feet ready for a fight.

"This isn't about you. What you did or didn't do. You want to sit there and watch? Then sit there and watch. Otherwise, put your fucking gloves on. The sooner we're done the sooner we can get away from here."

Volunteer

We entered each classroom, crumbling charcoal and partially burnt bodies distorted in poses of pain and silent screams lay twisted among the occasional perfectly unmarked, lifeless body that looked like it was in a peaceful sleep. The blackened walls and smoke blocked out the life beyond them, screams echoed inside my head; were they real or conjured up to torture me? It was hard to describe the smell. How do you describe burnt flesh? I had always assumed it would be like a barbecue smell, but it was more like a coal fire, when you first light it, mixed with stale body odour, and that strange smell you get from burnt hair. I was faint, but not sick. Maybe it was the smoke, maybe dehydration.

I picked up the bodies as if they were delicate pieces of furniture, cringing as my grip cracked burnt skin. How many bodies I lifted out I have no idea. I didn't count them. We lifted lifeless, rag-doll bodies taking care that we had a good hold, folding their arms across their chest so they didn't flop all over the place. Others were carefully formed sculptures rigid from the flames. Most took two people to carry out, but the hardest were the smallest children that only needed one of us to carry them. Carefully cradling them, as if they would dissolve in my arms, I controlled my breathing and was mindful of every step. I dropped to one knee and gently lay them down in the line, slowly rising to my feet and backing away.

Twenty-seven children were saved. Eighty-five classmates lay covered in brightly coloured blankets, masking the horrors beneath. Emotionally, I was dead. I had nothing to offer in the way of comfort, especially to the siblings that sat by the bodies, heads buried in hands to hide their sadness. My work here was done.

The drive back was long and quiet. We had nothing to say. I stared at my feet, everything was scattered in my head; flashes of faces, echoes of sounds. I was plagued by 'What if's?' and 'Why's?' I tried to connect the day's events to the civilized world. Was my civilization in any shape to judge? I was from a nation that killed each other over religions that a modern society no longer deemed important, or had much interest in. A divided Christian nation that acted anything but Christian. Regardless of the situation back home, it had nothing on this. Not even close.

Was this to be the small print of life that people interpreted as 'experience'? Was I to find an explanation in the 'everything happens for a reason' cliché? Well, excuse my ignorance, but I would never find the reasons why the fuck I had to go

Volunteer

through that. Was it so that I could recognise that I was alive? Right now the dead were the lucky ones, free from life's reasons and purposeful happenings.

We pulled into the clinic's courtyard, where Odette was waiting for us in tears. There was something not right about being involved in an atrocity like that and coming back empty-handed. As sadistic as it sounded, a few children writhing in pain would have been better than this lifeless, empty, silence. Michael was first off the 4x4, emotionally and physically drained; he put his arms around Odette, pulled her close and let go of the day's events. Tears rolled down his face and his body shook as he sobbed.

I didn't want to get off the truck. A day's work done? Time to shut off for the night and relax? Time for dinner and a few beers? I jumped off the back of the 4x4 and walked to door, Odette slipped away from Michael and moved to me with outstretched arms. My lip quivered, emotions swelling inside, threatening to break free. She reached for me and I stopped her with an open palm, unable to meet her eye. I couldn't comfort her; I wanted to hold her and tell her everything was fine, but it wasn't. I wasn't.

I strode to the door and barged through it, slamming it off the wall. I looked at no one, knowing fine rightly that the hospital staff were aware of what had happened, of my failures. I went to my room, tossed my bag on the bed and sat down. I took off the bloodied, charcoal-stained T-shirt and threw it into the corner of the room. I pulled at the laces of my boots and, once untied, yanked them off, one at a time with the same venom, and then threw them at the T-shirt. I pulled at my belt, opened my trousers and stepped out of them as they dropped.

Grabbing my towel from the back of my door handle, I marched down the hall to the washrooms. I had shed the protective shell of my death encrusted clothes and the cold air of the hospital bit at my naked skin.

My pace increased as pressure worked its way from my stomach. Choking it down, I slid up to open the door of the washrooms, ran across the cold tiles to the nearest cubicle and threw myself head first at the toilet bowl to wretch. I was as dry as the dirt outside, trying to throw up something, but instead just spitting and watching it dangle before dropping into the toilet. I wanted to get everything out of my system and flush it away as if it never existed. I wiped my mouth and stood tall, hands on

Volunteer

hips, taking deep breaths. Shaking my head in disappointment, I stared at the ceiling praying for some release.

I walked slowly to the showers dropping my towel on the floor outside. I turned on the first spigot, and waited out of the reach, as cold water bounced off the tiles and sprayed my feet. I stepped into the shower, still in my boxer shorts. I was weak and unsteady, the water too heavy for my body. I reached out for the wall to steady myself, but my arms buckled, forcing me to lean on my forearms, bowing my head onto the tiles as the water beat off my back and the charcoal and blood tracked its way down the drain.

I broke. My legs folded underneath my weight and sobs racked my body as the tears came. The falling water drowned my cries as I slid down the tiled walls bent double, emptiness gripping my stomach and curled into a foetal position, with my forearms and head still up against the wall. I lay powerless, motionless, sobs running into the stained water. Innocent blood washed away physically, but not mentally, down the drain.

Emmanuel found me, concerned by descriptions of my behaviour. I couldn't even move to recover my dignity, or to play out a false façade that I was unfazed and untouched by this. The shower hadn't done much to mask my emotional destruction as he stepped in and turned off the water.

"It was my fault, I killed them!" I spat.

Emmanuel crouched down and pulled me close, disregarding the fact I was soaked and that we were sitting in blood stained water. He held me tight as I tried to wrench free, undeserving of the attention and uncomfortable with this level of physical and emotional support.

"You saved twenty-seven. *They* killed eighty-five." Forcefully he held me, willing me to hear him.

"I took the gun. They wanted me," I whispered, throat closing. "I could have lifted more. I promised them I'd get them out, that I'd come back for them. They burned waiting for me."

I believed that, and to this day still do. A life-long regret. Regardless of who pulled the trigger, I failed to act fast enough.

"Never believe that. You did more than any of us. Very few of us could do what you did."

Volunteer

I don't know how long we sat. Odette came and shook out my towel, wrapping it around me as my body shook with cold, shock, and the aftermath of crying so hard. I had returned to my earlier paralysed state, unable to move. Odette crouched down and wiped her hand across my forehead and back over the crown of my head as she leaned over Emmanuel. Placing a drawn out kiss on the top of my head, she rested her head on mine and held my face in her hands. I couldn't bring myself to look at her, ashamed of my current state.

"He's OK. Delayed reaction due to shock," Emmanuel whispered "And Michael?"

Odette pulled herself reluctantly away.

"Much the same. Exhausted and sleeping in one of the wards."

Chapter 21: Seeking Revenge

I had often heard that people never sleep well after traumatic experiences, screaming out in to the night, reliving the ordeal, waking in a panicked sweat and being comforted by a loved one, reassured that it was all just a nightmare and that everything was okay. Well, that never happened. Truth of it was I slept like a log, physically and emotionally wrecked. I am sure my subconscious played through the day's events, but exhaustion cancelled out any form of unconscious physical reaction, I didn't even remember my head hitting the pillow.

I woke up like any other morning and went about my normal routine, more drained and subdued than the day before. I hadn't bothered though with breakfast, I wasn't hungry and couldn't face sitting in the small canteen talking about how I was feeling. I headed for the courtyard and there was Odette with food in her hand.

Volunteer

"You need to eat," she said. I took the food from her. "You sure you're up for this today? Maybe you need a day off?" I needed more than just a day off.

"I'm fine." I lifted my eyes from the floor, embarrassed by my display of vulnerability the day before. "Just need to get back out there and keep busy."

I took my usual place in the back of the truck, with a stern nod to Michael as I put my earphones in. I had music blasting through them before we pulled away, en-route to another emergency. It was clear morale was low; no one spoke, eyes distant, unable to change what had happened, we had accepted fate. This is what we did.

On the outside I was cool, collected, unfazed, as if the day before had never happened. I was far from content, but silent, with my own thoughts. On the inside I was screaming. Filled with the anger that plagued this country; I could kill someone. I was lost in my own head; thoughts of violence consumed the fear that once existed there. I knew it wouldn't take much to set me off. I wanted revenge, and I would push and push until I gave these fuckers a reason to kill me.

Suddenly, the 4x4 screeched to a halt, knocking us off-balance and threw us the other way as it flung into reverse. We had driven right into a fire fight. Through the dust cloud of panicked braking, puffs of dirt erupted as bullets dropped around us, hitting the truck.

"Is anyone hit? Is everyone OK?" Michael shouted in English, before repeating himself in Amharic.

We tried to see where the shooting was coming from, but my eyes had locked on to something else. I wasn't sure - nor did I care - if it was a dead rebel or dead soldier, but they had something of interest; an AK47.

I pushed past Michael and jumped off the 4x4 as it was reversing, almost falling on my face. I scrambled over to the weapon and heard Michael screaming at me as I grabbed the rifle, searching the previous owner's vest and pockets for magazines, and finding three. I pulled at the bolt-action with my right hand, realising it took more effort than I expected, and let it snap back and checked the safety. Thank God for computer games.

Pulling myself to my feet, I walked around the corner without hesitation, or thoughts for my

Volunteer

own safety. I lifted the gun, tucking it into my shoulder, almost day-dreaming the scene in slow motion as I took aim and squeezed the trigger. I sprayed the full magazine at the rebels and wasn't expecting the recoil, which pushed me back a few steps as I fired. Most of the magazine went into the air as I dropped to one knee beside the gable wall of a house.

'Well, that was embarrassing,' I thought.

Certainly wasn't how I expected to enter the battle field, but there was a lot to be said about the lack of recoil when pushing the R1 button on a Play Station controller. I fumbled, trying to replace the empty magazine with a full one, standing in plain view, using my leg to take the weight of the gun and hold it steady as the new magazine clicked into place. I pulled at the bolt-action. This was not how I had played this war scene in my head, there was nothing cool about what I was doing right now.

The Ethiopian soldiers who joined me were, I imagined, laughing at the stupid white kid as I stood across the street. I must have looked ridiculous. This time I fired off the full clip in short bursts. For more precision, I rested the stock on my shoulder, but leant into the recoil, walked forward and aimed in the direction of the rebels. I wasn't much better, but maintaining composure in front of these guys was more important, so I took it seriously.

The rebels made off through the streets, out the back of the buildings they had commandeered, as the Ethiopian soldiers progressed towards them. Ignoring Michael's calls, I followed, wanting a closer look. Up the hill, the rebel convoy was loading up retreating troops and a 4x4 with a mounted machine gun was shooting down the street to cover them. I stood contemplating my next move. Go for the machine gunner or call it quits? Without warning the 4x4 exploded. I dived to the nearest wall for cover, dropping to my knees.

Was not expecting that at all!

The retreating vehicles tried to squeeze past the burning wreckage as others retreated on foot. We had the upper hand. I watched as Ethiopian soldiers broke off to the right, down a side street, to cut off the retreat and found myself running behind them, in fact behind an Ethiopian soldier holding an RPG on his shoulder. Here's hoping he didn't trip. Why couldn't I have found one of those lying around instead of the AK47? I held my rifle upright, trying to change the magazine on the move, with little success.

Volunteer

I discarded the empty magazine and ran into the first gap I came to; I wasn't about to run the entire length of the town and gunfire echoed along the road as a rebel truck sped along and there was a 4x4 approaching fast and I tried to gauge how far away it was. I remained calm and focused on putting the magazine in as I hid behind a building. Was this magazine damaged? Damn thing wouldn't go in; I was going to miss out. I tried again as I jogged along the alleyway. Damn! Of all the people running about, someone had to run in to me. I slid down the wall and fell onto my side. I tried to gather the magazine that the idiot had knocked out of my hand. I looked up to get an apology. I wasn't going to get it.

I felt sick with the rush of fear and adrenaline as the equally terrified LF rebel, who was about the same age as me, kicked out at my face. I tried to roll out of the way but his boot heel struck my left shoulder, just missing my face, and I threw the magazine at him.

Yes, that's right - gun in one hand and I threw the fucking bullets away with the other!

I hauled myself to my knees, dropped the rifle and jumped on top of him. What the fuck was I doing? Why wasn't I running? What was I trying to do, arrest him?

He reached for his weapon and I grabbed at his stretching hand, his free arm swung up as he tried to unseat me. His elbow connected with my face and I rolled back, taking his head with me as I pulled him into a headlock. He clenched my T-shirt and blindly slapped an open hand into my face as he tried to loosen my grip. Growling at each other like dogs, I wrapped my legs around one of his; the strong little bastard was pulled away, almost lifting me off the ground he slammed a clenched fist into the side of my head. He slipped out of the headlock and I grabbed at his dark green shirt. The buttons popped off as I pulled my body off the ground and tackled him to the floor. This was going nowhere fast and I had nothing to restrain him with. I had to either knock him out or kill him. With what though?

I dropped my forearm onto his throat to choke him out, and he grabbed the side of my head and slammed it into the wall beside us.

Fuck did that hurt!

White specks danced across my eyes, I was stunned, my reactions slowed as he slammed my head into the wall for the second time. This time I dropped, the energy knocked out of me, and he slid

Volunteer

from under me, kicking me away as I unsuccessfully, grappled for his ankles. I rolled over to see him grab his rifle off the ground and I lay there, too exhausted to beg for my life. He sluggishly stood, tired from rolling around and handing my ass to me. He held the rifle with both hands pointing down at me and I screamed at him.

"Go on then, fucking shoot!" I jumped at the sound of gunfire, shutting my eyes and covering my head as I rolled into a ball. Did he miss or was that just a warning? I was sure if he had shot me I would have felt it. I slowly uncurled, opening my eyes. His lifeless body lay angled against the wall, a blood splattered shadow marked where he once stood.

I pulled myself into a seated position, reached across and trailed the AK47 towards me by its strap. Unsteadily, I got to my feet, hugging the wall to get away from the body, worried he might grab me or I would fall on him. I had seen way too many horrors where the bad guy, despite being gunned down, still managed to make one last attempt. I picked up the magazine I had thrown and watched as his blood drained from him. I backed off slowly, thankful I couldn't see his face because the mess of him from the back didn't paint a pretty picture.

I touched my forehead. It wasn't bleeding, but it was sore, scraped and swelling up. I made my way along the alleyway without looking back. I felt nothing for the guy after what had just happened. It was him or me.

I picked a spot at the end of an alleyway by the main escape road, not wanting to look out and give away my position. I wanted the element of surprise. What if I had missed the entire convoy?

"Come on!" I growled, as I fought with the magazine, clicking it into place and snapping the bolt before positioning it on my shoulder. I aimed at a rebel 4x4 that was metres away and I screamed, forcing all my anger out through my teeth and through the trigger. Rage, from my determination to kill, fuelled every bullet.

Gunfire erupted along the length of the road; bullets sprayed and blew out every window, and punctured the entire side of the vehicle. The rear passengers were either slumped in the back of the trailer or flipped off onto the road by the force of ammunition ripping through them, they crashed to the ground, bodies twisted. The driver lost control and smashed into the deep concrete sewer channel that ran along the side of the road; this was too good to pass up. This was it. I would get my kill. This was *my* kill.

The last magazine felt lighter than the others. Not sure if that made it easier, or if I was getting more efficient at reloading. I walked towards the wreck, rifle dropped from aim, but finger poised over the trigger, ready to go if anything moved. I was wired. It didn't matter what, if it moved, it died. A rebel, a bird, a leaf. I contemplated the kill. Should I walk around the vehicle and kill any survivors one at a time, or just spray the vehicle with bullets and hope the fuel tank would explode like a movie scene. I didn't know where the fuel tank was, so fuck it I would spray it with bullets and hope for the best. Due to the time wasted on my usual over thinking, the decision was made for me as the 4x4 exploded. I threw up my arm, turning my face away from the heat. Another couple of steps and I would have demonstrated my ineptitude as a fire guard.

The burning wreckage stirred mixed emotions; I wanted to cheer like a mad man as they burned, dance in victory, firing the rest of the magazine high into the air. But I didn't. I screamed. Unconsciously and without control. Not a war cry or in pain, just noise; anger, frustration, failure, and doubt surged from the soles of my feet, through my tensed body and blasted from my mouth, echoing through the streets until I stopped, light-headed and breathlessness. I needed that.

I can't be sure that I got a kill, but I was involved in the destruction that had unfolded, just metres away. I had emptied a full magazine into the affray and there had been no signs of life when the 4x4 had crashed. It wasn't enough. I wanted these to be the squad that hit the school, I wanted to stand over them and see the terror in their face, for them to recognise me from the day before. But, it wasn't to be. I would have to let this one go and wait for the next opportunity. I stood close enough to feel the scorching heat of the flames, my imagination conjured up bullets shattering the window screen and ripping the driver and passenger apart. I played the scene over and over in my head in slow motion, to convince myself that was how it happened.

I was alone on the street. The Ethiopian soldiers were long gone in their pursuit. The rifle hung from my arm, resting down the side of my body and I could feel its heat through my combats. Now that the rush was over my arm muscles burned from wielding this great chunk of metal and wood, and I was convinced my shoulder would be bruised. Every bullet was like a punch; fine for a few shots, but thirty odd times per magazine hurt. I went down

Volunteer

the hill, through the gap I had come out of, and discarded the rifle.

The novelty was wearing off as I made my way back to the MAA 4x4s. The crew was tending to the injured close to the spot I had originally picked up the rifle. There were ten bodies being attended to, had they been there the whole time? I didn't remember passing them.

"What the fuck was that?" Michael shouted, coming towards me.

"What was what?" I tried to play it cool, but knew I was in the wrong.

"You're a fucking soldier now? Got your big army boots on with your fucking gun? What the fuck, man!" I followed Michael, who was handing out wrapping.

"I'm sick of standing about doing nothing," I argued, thinking it was a perfectly reasonable explanation. Hoping he would leave it at that.

"This is what we do." He stopped and faced me, pointing to the volunteers attending to the wounded and dead. "You think I don't want to pick up a gun and take those fuckers down? That's not what we're about, man. They fight for their stupid cause and we pick up the pieces. We're bringing hope to the injured, letting them know that someone gives a shit about them."

I stood in silence. I had nothing to come back with.

"So, yeah, you kill one or two of them," Michael spat. "Then what? You think that's going to make up for yesterday? Killing eighty odd of them does not even the score. All you've fucking done is put us in the shit and made us a target. This isn't about you. You want to play toy soldiers, then go ahead, but you won't do it with us around."

I stood embarrassed and ashamed, not because of what I had done, but because he was right. I was putting their lives in danger. But, fuck. I was furious. I wanted to pick up the gun and keep going; it wasn't about trying to even the score.

I walked over to the 4x4 to get a bottle of water, walking around the injured. I struggled with my conscience. I had killed; not a rebel, but another human being. The death of the rebel in the alleyway was my fault. I had to have killed at least the passenger - and possibly the driver - in the rebel truck. But, since I could barely use a gun I tried to rationalise that I couldn't have been that accurate.

Volunteer

Did they veer off the road and crash because I wounded the driver and he lost control? Surely that made killing them my fault? But did I even hit the 4x4? What if I had hadn't tackled the rebel in the alleyway? Would he have killed me or just run off?

I was losing a grip on my mind. How could I start helping these people if I had contributed to their misery and death? How much of a hypocrite would that make me?

Once we lifted the injured to the clinic the afternoon was quiet. Michael said nothing more about earlier. In fact, we had barely spoken at all. We were dropped close to Hell Hole village and together ambled silently in the punishing sun. This time I had remembered my book and sat on the edge reading, hoping to escape from everything. I immersed myself into the life of a retired FBI agent helping to track down a serial child killer. Michael tapped my arm with a bottle of water.

"Listen man, I'm sorry," Michael said. "I understand what you're going through and why you did it. Fuck, I'd love to shoot some of those fuckers, but we need to stick together and look after our own. It's the whole reason I didn't do my national service and chose to volunteer here. To make a real difference, instead of being part of the problem.

Now if they were to hit us, and we had no way out, you better believe I'd come out fighting."

"I thought all this was over."

"Nah. This is Africa. People represent their tribe first and the country second. Whatever tribe has the most guns, rules the country. Works for a while. The western world sends aid to help the new government in the hope they make a real change. It starts with unity and big promises. But then they get greedy. Promises get broken until another tribe stands up and takes them on. It's constant. The irony is that Africa has some of the richest countries in the world in terms of minerals, resources, diamonds and shit. The western world bleeds the country dry and then gives it aid to cover up its guilt. When war breaks out the locals are looked upon as savages, animals. What's more uncivilized? A man who is fighting to protect his family, fighting for food, education and medical care? Or, the man who rapes the country of another, stealing its wealth and forcing it into war? War pays better than peace."

"So, what does that make us?" I asked

"Don't know. Some say humanitarians. Back home we'll be admired as pillars of the community. Our countries will view us as a statistic of their

Volunteer

generosity. To us, it depends on the reasons for doing it. I'd say we're opportunists. Personally, I do this to make myself feel good and for the free trip abroad. To make my life worth more, so I can live out the rest of it guilt-free. Telling myself that I made a difference."

What was I looking for? What did I want from this trip? I didn't want any of this. I did volunteer – well, not exactly for this, but still. I wasn't contracted to stay, but I had. What had I become? I had come from digging foundation holes, building a community, to being part of the problem. From standing on the rim of civilization and sanity, to falling over the edge into chaos and hate. I had lost sight of who I was. My principles, my morals, and emotions. Without fear, I no longer cared about my own safety, or anyone else. Is that what this country was? A place where people accepted the short comings of death as a way of life?

The pages of my book lay open and unread, the words were visible, but I couldn't string them together into sentences or follow the story. I couldn't concentrate, and again I wondered why I was here.

Starvation and war, the third world's alternative to the first world's greed and endless searching for happiness. The difference was our fate was in our hands, theirs was in somebody else's. All the issues and bullshit from back home did not compare to this. Ours was a so-called war, fought on force-fed truths to try and justify a cause. History was often rewritten by the narrow-minded, supposedly for people who would be abused and forgotten in the end. Ruled by corrupt councillors and terrorists, who signed their own government pay checks.

A life of trying to get one over on the rivals, taking as much as you could for yourself, while endlessly whining about what the other side had that you didn't. We had to have two of everything to keep the bigots and their representatives quiet and divided. Communities were often destroyed and then they would complain that they lived in a shit-hole.

Yet, here were people with fuck-all and they were perfectly fine with that. I may have lost my way and become a savage, but I would rather be appreciated by a foreign people for trying to fight for something real – even if I continued to fall short – than to be a nobody whining about things that I didn't want and meant nothing when I got them.

Chapter 22: Day 1

Things were spiralling out of control, the braver I became, the more the situations escalated. I had crossed a line and coming back from that was impossible, the damage was already done, not just to my reputation, but to my way of thinking.

We headed northwest towards the border, close to the town of Badme, one of the focal points of a territorial dispute since both Eritrea and Ethiopia laid claim to it. There were plenty of refugee camps for a group of people that both nations recognized as voters, but that rejected all responsibility for them.

We visited a small medical outpost that was originally home to a missionary for children orphaned by the conflict. More fucking children. Not exactly something I needed right now.

The drive had been long and my ass was numb from being driven on unforgiving roads. The only decent part of the road was the small stretch of bridge, over a river of dust, as we drove up the main street of this little village. There were two long buildings, either side of the road, both decent quality – well, the best we had seen on our way here - although aged and badly patched up, much the same as the hotel back in Dessie. We pulled up in front of a well-kept white 4x4, a year or two old, with large, iconic, red crosses plastered all over it.

"I wonder what they do?" I pointed to the truck, struggling to straighten as something clicked in the base of my back. My face twisted, not from pain, but from the uncomfortable sound that a spine shouldn't make.

"You alright?" Michael inquired, his face twisted to mirror mine.

"Aye. Old age, just."

"Old age my ass!" Michael laughed as he waved for me to go into one of the buildings with him.

It may have resembled the hotel in Dessie from the outside, but inside it was more like one of the houses we had built. Dark, with a smell that was somewhere between musty antiques, and cold damp concrete. We walked along a thin corridor and into a

Volunteer

small office; the furniture was basic, with paperwork covering most of the surfaces. The sound of children in organised, playful chaos came from somewhere in the building.

There were a few people in the office, most notably two other white people, which was kind of a relief. It was nice to think that the same shit had happened to them, albeit an assumption.

"And this is Chris." Michael reached out to bring me into the conversation. I reached forward to shake the woman's hand first, a petite brunette with hair tied back, and then the guy's massive farmer hand; your typical surfer, with the tan and the shaggy unbrushed blond hair. They identified themselves as Jenna and Tim.

"Where are you guys from?" I enquired.

"Canada." Jenna was awkward and direct, which wasn't the Canadian way. They were always a real friendly type and chatty, based on a few holidays I had taken to there. Okay, I didn't know every Canadian, but something was wrong here. Since we had come in the two of them hadn't moved from the desk they were leaning against, and their helpers didn't appear very helpful. My mind whirred, trying to think of a way out or to figure out what the hell was going on. Michael left to find the manager, since it was late and we were going to need somewhere to stay for the night.

"So, you guys been here long?" I tried to assess whether they were just shy or if something was wrong. "Who are you with?"

"We're with a medical agency that monitors and visits orphanages," Jenna replied.

Again, Tim didn't flinch, intently inspecting his feet, not uttering a word, which aroused my suspicions. Fuck it, I'd just ask.

"You guys OK?"

A commotion outside interrupted Jenna's shaking exhale.

I marched back down the corridor to the exit and our 4x4, knowing full well that Tim, Jenna and their crew were following me outside. A number of men stood around our 4x4, our driver was arguing with a man who was pulled at his arm, trying to haul him out of his seat.

Everyone was a lot older than me and I was slightly intimidated, worried my authority wouldn't carry, but that wasn't going to stop me.

Volunteer

"What the fuck?"

As always, I didn't fully assess the situation, I just ran in and shouted my mouth off, I had never said two words to our driver, but he was one of us and no one laid hands on our team.

"Get your fucking hands off him!" I ordered, but a hand gun pushed towards my face stopped me, I was out of my depth. I dealt with it in the manner that was newly typical of me. "Get that gun out of my fucking face!"

I swiped at the gun as the gunman stepped back, holding the weapon sideways 'gangster' style, still pointed at my head.

"Who the fuck are you guys? What do you want?" I regretted coming out here without Michael. I was sure to make the situation a lot worse. All these guys had guns.

"They're locals. They aren't going to let you leave." Tim the surfer finally spoke up. But if ever there was a time to become the front-runner of a conversation, it wasn't now. I spun round glaring.

"What? What you mean we can't leave?"

Thankfully, Michael arrived just in time to hear my question.

"What's going on?" Michael was equally dumbfounded by the number of armed men surrounding our 4x4, which kind of reassured me that I hadn't offended someone, and this wasn't normal.

"If they let us go, they are dead. With us here they will have a chance to live," Tim explained, obviously nervous, his hands shaking. This time Jenna stood back.

"What shit are you talking? You knew about this when we arrived and you said fuck-all? You prick!" I lunged at Tim, but Michael stepped in front of me. The guys around the truck were getting restless.

"Everyone calm down. What's the problem here? What do they want?" Michael took over the conversation, with more of a cool head.

"Just over the bridge, there is an LF patrol and further up the road from here there is another," Tim explained. "They have no way out. They are trapped in the middle. The LF over the bridge will push through here and those that try to escape will run straight into the other patrol. With us here, the

Volunteer

LF won't move unless they have to." Tim lowered himself on to the step, running his hands through his hair revealing, a rather large, tanned forehead. How the hell did it tan with all that hair in the way?

"Well, we're white so they're not going to kill us. No offence Michael," I said without actually thinking. I had never seen him in danger because of his colour. To me he was just an American.

"Oh fuck man, none taken."

"You're right, they won't kill you, but they will kill your crew," Tim said, as an extra bonus.

"So, we come here to help these guys and they hold us hostage? We just sit here 'till this standoff is over?" I was becoming increasingly frustrated with being stuck somewhere unfamiliar because of betrayal at the hands of people we had tried to help.

"They allowed one of our trucks to leave and get supplies this morning, so they should be back with military help in a day and a half, max," Jenna joined in.

"Shit. Well, I guess we wait it out." Michael shrugged, ever calm and understanding. In fairness, there wasn't much we could do.

"How do you know your truck will make it?" I asked. "Even at that, why the fuck are the military going to help?"

This was all a bit far-fetched, I wanted something more concrete than the crap I was being fed. "We've been looking after injured Ethiopian soldiers who were chased here by the LF patrol across the bridge," Tim finally came clean. So that was the reason for this situation.

After all the talk of how the military had their own people, their own supplies, here they were using us. We lived by the rules of separating ourselves from them as we cleared up their mess. They broke that rule and pulled us into their mess. Rather than stay and fight and do their job, they hid like cowards in an orphanage. I slid down the front of our 4x4. This had the potential to become another school incident.

"Unfortunately, there are no beds left, but you do have your own room. I wouldn't think of trying to escape in the night, the trucks are guarded," Jenna said. Anger had subsided. This couldn't be any worse. I was hot, sweaty, covered in dust, and really pissed off, but too tired to amount to anything useful. Without fail, there is always something to make it worse.

Volunteer

"We don't have enough water or food, so use what you have sparingly."

Thank you Jenna. Fucking typical.

Chapter 23: Day 2 Realisation

I wandered aimlessly about outside. Jenna sat on the ground in a circle of children, rolling a ball between them. I slumped against the 4x4 watching with Michael. The kids enjoyed the game, but I thought it pointless, maybe it was just my competitive nature, but what were the rules or the objectives of this game? Was there even a winner?

I was grumpy, my back stiff from sleeping on a concrete floor with no blanket and just my bag for a pillow. I was tired, too. Half the night spent plotting ways to escape, the other half imagining spiders the size of dinner plates crawling all over me and in my mouth.

When I finally got to sleep, the cold had woken me. I had tried to rub warmth into my frozen arms before pulling them inside my T-shirt, folding them around my body, and surprisingly I fell asleep that way.

Volunteer

"Did you sleep well?" A cheery Tim marched out of the building.

"Wonderfully," I replied sarcastically. After his silence yesterday, and with me not being a morning person anyway, I wasn't in the mood for his shit.

"Sorry, just trying to lighten the situation."

"So, I get the possible food shortage, but why is there no water? No taps or a pump or anything?" My mouth was as dry as bone, with that nasty morning taste.

"There is a pump just up the road. Two guys went to check it out and never came back. They shot another two people dead just over there in the road when we tried to get water. It's too dangerous man. We also lost a few people who tried to escape under the bridge, the LF gunned them down."

Familiar blood patterns stained the excuse for a road. How did we not notice them on the way in? That would have been a warning sign and a half. I was restless, stuck for something to do; my iPod battery was dead and I didn't want to read.

I was a prisoner, allowed out in the yard to walk around and kick the dirt about, but there was no escape. Selfishly, I knew I could have left. I considered it, already fed up with hanging around and tired of entertaining kids. The LF were here for blood and they were going to get it regardless. I knew Michael was thinking the same. We were fucked. Michael, Jenna, Tim and I would live, but we would be forced to either abandon the compound to the sounds of a massacre or worse, we would be forced to watch it happen.

"Oh shit!" Tim burst out.

"What?" I sprang up.

"Come back! Terug te kom!" Tim screamed at a woman who was running away from us along the bridge with her two children. I sprinted past Tim. If I got close enough they might not shoot. As she stepped off the bridge a 4x4 pulled in front of her; the woman froze, released the children's hands and screamed at them. They turned and fled towards me as she sacrificed herself, a shot rang out and she dropped to the ground.

The older of the children ran back to his mother, while the confused, tearful, little girl stumbled towards me. I grabbed her in mid stride and ran for the boy, but it was too late. A short burst of gunfire cut the air and he fell to the ground. I

Volunteer

stopped, almost squeezing the life out of the screaming child in my arms, and watched one of the rebels use his hand to mime shooting a gun at me and Tim, who had arrived at my side.

"I'm going to kill that fucker," I glared down the far end of the bridge. I didn't know if it was all talk, but I was fed up with this shit. Always on the side that was losing people. I stormed back towards the compound to the waiting crowd. Jenna tried to loosen the child's vice-like grip from around my neck.

"We need to do something!" I shouted to Michael.

"Like what?" Michael challenged.

"I don't know, but I can't stand this shit anymore. We can't ignore what's going on here or what's going to happen."

"Keep your voice down," Michael growled.

"Why?" I tried to spark the ever calm Michael in to action. "There must be something we can do?"

"If we had a bus we could block the windows and drive out of here," Tim offered.

"Have we got a bus?" I enquired, enthusiastically.

"No." Tim dropped his head.

"Why would you say that? How is that helping?" I shook my head; at least he was making more of an effort than Michael, albeit useless.

"There is another other idea that the soldiers put forward yesterday, but it's suicide," Tim offered, nervously.

"I hope it's an improvement on your invisible bus," I warned.

Tim explained the plan with Jenna's help, like a comedy duo or one of those annoying couples that finish each other's sentences. The Ethiopian army would be here tomorrow, so that meant the bridge patrol - as we were calling the ones across the bridge - would drive through the town and flush out the compound, forcing everyone into the flanking patrol.

It was reported the patrols usually partied at night with alcohol, drugs, and music blasting. The macho gunfire either was intended to keep everyone awake or maintain a level of fear throughout the

Volunteer

compound. The plan was to attack the flanking patrol.

We would take their supplies, weapons and 4x4s and when the bridge patrol came through we would hit them from both sides of the road. Would it work? I suspected the only chance of this working was if Hollywood was directing it with some CGI, but what other choice did we have?

"You'll need to build barricades at both ends of the compound to at least slow down the attacks" Michael said, finally contributing to the conversation, "and they would provide useful protection and to cover up what we're planning. I saw some barrels and shit lying around and corrugated iron sheets." Probably the most do-able and realistically achievable suggestion yet.

"That won't really slow them down though." I didn't want to be negative, on possibly the best suggestion of the day, but it wasn't enough.

"Oh it will. They just won't see the whole picture." This was the Michael I had pushed for. I knew he had something amazing planned: mines, homemade rockets and explosives.

"So, what is it?" I had to know what was being developed.

"Well, we build a frame and nail the corrugated iron sheets to them, then attach it to long posts and bury the posts in the barrels full of sand. It will act as our curtain. Once we set that up right across the entrance, we dig out a foot deep trench and we take the junk heap motors over there and push them into the trench and fill it back in. You can guarantee they are going to hit that wall at speed. If they don't hit the cars, they'll nose dive into the trench. Be a fucking pile up."

Okay, so there were no explosives or rockets, but that would be genius - if it worked.

"We'd better get to work then," Jenna suggested.

Chapter 24: Day 2 Implementation

With such a large group it didn't take us long to construct Michael's barricades. The locals did most of the work as we were confined to the shade of the buildings on Jenna's orders. With the threat of the water shortage, none of us needed to collapse right now. This was a struggle for me and I had to be told two or three times to stop what I was doing. It wasn't really in my nature to sit about doing nothing while others were working, but Jenna put a stop to it with a bit of light comedy, she marched over to me, emphasizing her footsteps, and led me by the scruff towards the building, the children applauded and laughed, all smiles.

I'd never been in a situation like this before, left to sit alone and gather my thoughts, which was probably for the best; God knows what my mind would conjure up. My time was interrupted by Ila, the three-year old girl I had lifted off the bridge yesterday, who still wasn't talking. She didn't come to me because I was her saviour, it was just that my lap was a free space. I sat on the floor, with my back to the wall, and watched as she toddled over and dropped onto my crossed legs, clutching onto a colouring book page. She was oblivious to me. I watched the concentration on her face as she scribbled with a red crayon, with complete disregard for keeping inside the lines. While she was quiet I leaned back and closed my eyes.

I was woken up by gentle shaking. Ila was asleep on my lap and I struggled with my dried out contacts, blinking forcefully. Tim was hanging over me.

"What?" I leaned away from him.

"The soldiers are calling everyone out to see how many of us there are and what weapons we have for this attack," Tim whispered, as Ila squirmed.

"I don't think that means us. We're the hostages remember. What the fuck do we know about fighting?" I wasn't sure Tim understood my sarcasm. He lifted Ila off me and handed her to a local woman. I picked myself up, reflective of an old man with bad knees, using the wall to steady

Volunteer

myself as I pushed up. My legs were cramped from sitting so long, and I staggered out of the shade.

A large group had gathered and were discussing the plans. Michael filled me in as one of the soldiers spoke. The army would take the lead and attack directly at the heart of the flanking LF patrol once the partying started. As soon as they scattered, the rest of us would pick them off. There were twelve to sixteen troops, fully armed, with three 4x4s - two of which had mounted guns of sorts. This plan was as appealing as replacing toilet roll with sandpaper.

"We're not actually going to get involved in this are we?" To be honest, I asked, not out of fear, but to take Michael's lead. If he said no, then that was fine. If he said yes, well, I didn't know how I'd feel about that. Excited, anxious, terrified? I would deal with it anyway.

"I'm not," Michael said, walking back towards the MMA 4x4, arms folded. "They can kill me if they want, but I'm staying here."

"I am." Tim fidgeted with adrenaline and confidence. I was surprised; I never suspected he would have had a violent streak, or maybe I was concerned that he wasn't the sharpest tool in the box.

"They're going to need medics," he said, which was a fair point.

"Better get our packs then." I could do this; I had done it, since joining Michael and the crew. It would be fine; I would be part of the operation, albeit in a small way.

As I gathered up my bag, my mind was not in the right place, I crammed it with everything that would fit.

"Just take wrapping," Tim said, as he walked towards me, trying to keep me focused. "That's going to be too heavy and there is a good chance we may have to run for our lives." I never gave the guy much credit due to our previous engagements, but he had his head switched on when it came to the medical side of things.

"Here"-Tim passed me a handgun-"I was told to give you this." It was a lot bigger and heavier than I had expected it to be.

"It's a Z88. You have a fifteen-shot magazine, but you only have one, so be careful. It's a semi-automatic. The button on the top, above your thumb, is the safety. So, push it down and you're ready to shoot," Tim explained.

"Fuck do I need this for? How do you know how to use one of these?" Holding the gun at arm's length, pointing it to the ground, I was expecting it to go off. Not exactly the professional gun slinger I was trying to be a few days ago.

"You need it for obvious reasons, and I know about it because the guy who gave me mine told me," Tim shrugged.

What the fuck were the obvious reasons? We weren't to be involved in this fight. We were the medics, behind everyone, at the back of everything. We should be getting met on the way back, because we would be so far behind the fighting.

"Plus, we need to put some oil on our faces, like war paint. If they shine a torch on us their bullets will be like moths to a flame."

Was I being punished for picking that gun up the other day? Fuck that. It didn't matter what happened before or what might happen. Tomorrow didn't mean a thing if this plan didn't work. This was the here and the now and I knew what I had to do. I had to take my bag, take the gun and put on my war paint and stop shaking if possible. Was it fear or adrenaline? Probably both. I had to do this, simple as that. Before, I had acted out. It was all about me. But not this time. This was for everyone else. I stood motionless. My mind raced on ahead with the soldiers that just left. When the hell did it get so dark? Ethiopia always got dark really early, around seven o'clock. It was never a gradual sunset, the sun just dropped out of the sky and it was dark. Yeah, I was panicking.

"We've got to go." Tim waved me on, and we disappeared into the dark, away from the safety of the compound.

I followed the feet of the person in front of me, holding my gun with both hands like a detective from an American police drama. I had too much oil on; I looked like a tangoed air-hostess and had the odour of a rusty paint tin. I heard the music, chanting, and gunfire, but was that the army gunfire or the rebels? Maybe it would be over by the time we got there. They were close, I was surprised they hadn't heard us talking about the plan from the compound.

Oh shit, where did everyone go? Where was I supposed to be? I wanted to call out, but I was afraid I would be heard. I got down on one knee and

Volunteer

squinted, willing my eyes to catch a glimpse of something.

Then, all hell broke loose.

Strobe-light gunfire bursts lit up the darkness. Shadowed silhouettes ran against the back drop of the fire. Two 4x4s started up and then more gunfire. What do I do? Did I start shooting at the silhouettes? Stay here? Move in? How would I know who was who? Was I supposed to be shooting? My eyes picked up a movement from something. What was it? It was getting closer, maybe it was Tim.

"Tim?" I forced out a whisper.

Oh shit, it wasn't Tim. Someone ran straight for me. Fuck it, kill or be killed. I raised the gun to where I needed to shoot.

"Freeze! Don't move!" I screamed. What was I, a fucking policeman? My mind yelled 'shoot!' as my hands shook. Well, I did warn him. I tried to pull the trigger, but it didn't move. It was stuck. Bastards gave me a faulty gun. Oh fuck, the safety. Just as I figured it out, the wind left my lungs as I was smashed to the ground, both hands still holding firmly to the gun, if I lost it, I was never finding it again. Punches came from everywhere.

Was there more than one attacker, or had he got four arms? I covered my head, trying to knee, kick, and roll him off me. I grabbed a hold of him by the throat and hit out with the gun. Again, and again, I struck hard until I was bundled over.

Something else hit me from the right hand side and I fell on my face. Scrambling to get up, he was right beside me. One arm held me in a headlock and the other punched me repeatedly to the top of my head. I desperately flailed and shuffled to get to my knees, and tried to break free. Eventually, I fell back and kicked out to get some distance between us while my thumb flicked the gun safety off. As my finger twitched, the shot vibrated up my arm. Then the weight of the silent body dropped on top of me. I lay there. I couldn't breathe as I wrestled my hand still holding the gun from between us, flinging it away. My lungs opened. What should I do? Should I run? Should I help him? Was that stupid? Shoot him and then nurse him back to health?

I gently rolled the body off me. There was nothing. No groans, no twitching limbs, just silence. So, I sat with my arms folded, hunched over crossed legs, waiting for a sign of life. I couldn't hear if he was breathing above my own forced intake, I scanned around, first for the LF camp, then to get my bearings. Not sure if we won or not. I couldn't

Volunteer

tell the difference between celebration cries and fighting screams. Either way, no one was looking for me so I wouldn't be missed. I lifted myself to my feet. Fuck it. Back to the compound.

The journey back took no time, a hell of a lot shorter than when we left. I walked through the barricade. Back up must have arrived, as there were three armed 4x4s in the middle of the road.

"Chris!" The cry came from Michael. He, Tim, and Jenna ran towards me.

"Where have you been? The plan worked, they got the weapons and the trucks." Tim filled me in on the events.

What about leaving no man behind? Fucking left me out there on my own.

"You
OK? You hurt?" Michael was concerned.

"No ..." I was spaced out. Not dehydrated or in shock, just my head was somewhere else. I wanted to find a quiet spot, sit and relax. To come down off the adrenalin high. What time was it?

"You look pale and that's a serious amount of blood on your T-shirt." Michael glanced at Tim and Jenna, gauging their reaction.

"Yeah? Yeah ... that's what kept me. I found a casualty, so was working on him ... Yeah. I think he might have died. Left him up there. We can go back tomorrow and pick him up maybe…" All three stood in silence. Did they know I was lying? How would they know? I was paranoid.

"Where is your gun?" Tim asked. Why did he care about that stupid gun?

"I put it down somewhere. When I was trying to help that guy… the one who was bleeding. I forgot to lift it, probably still there."

It may well have been, but I wasn't going back for it. Jenna let go of Ila's hand; she had hidden behind Tim and I hadn't noticed her. She ran towards me, holding her colouring paper and crayon in one hand, the other reached out for mine. I couldn't deal with her right now. I didn't want to take her hand. Why couldn't she stay with the other children? I wanted to be left alone. But to halt rising suspicions I took her hand. I didn't want her to start crying. How awkward would that be?

Volunteer

So, Ila and I walked towards my temporary holding cell, the sounds of accusation and whispered concerns behind me.

Chapter 25: Day 3 Execution

Tim woke me again, a little harsher this time, and Ila was asleep in my lap. I was convinced I hadn't slept at all. The night's events still played in my head. This time Tim's repetitive whining and shaking woke up Ila, too, and I pushed her off me to the waiting hands of Jenna.

"What do you want? Speak slower." The politeness of my morning self took charge.

"They're coming," Tim said. He hadn't stopped shaking me, though I was awake now. "They are about to cross the bridge."

"The army?" I shrugged his hand off me.

"No, the LF, the bridge patrol. Come on!" Tim took off out of the room as I scrapped to my feet. This news was enough to fully wake me up.

Volunteer

I ran outside. Tim stood waiting by our 4x4 and handed me a rifle. It looked like an AK47, but not one I knew. My knowledge of weapons was limited to first person shooting games.

"Here, take this"-he handed me a petrol bomb-"you know what it is?"

"Please. This is my country's weapon of choice. I know a petrol bomb when I see it." Cocky, although I had never made, or thrown one before.

"Molotov cocktail, actually," Tim said with a smirk.

"You say highway, we say motorway. Same fucking thing." I followed him across the road. There was urgency in the air as our lookouts ran, and we sprinted to the safety of the buildings. I hunched by the wall and faced away from the barricade, listening to the hum of whatever was approaching. And it was coming in fast, just as Michael predicted it would. Where was Michael? I hadn't seen him at all; normally he would have run around shouting at me.

An explosion of noise interrupted my train of thought. Metal, glass, scrapping, crunching, screams, banging, gunfire, every noise of war played a chaotic melody. Two 4x4s smashed into the barricade, disturbing the resting place of the retired vehicles as they flipped into the air, crushing into the unmoving ground. Two other 4x4s followed with equal force. I stood like a rabbit caught in headlights. They had broken through the barricade; that wasn't supposed to happen. Someone grabbed my hand briefly, then slapped my back and ran past me. The petrol bomb I held had been lit. Panicking, I followed Tim's lead and I launched my device straight at one of the overturned 4x4s. It smashed against its target and flames erupted from it.

I stood back in horror as bodies leaped out of the vehicles, kicking and punching the air to throw the flames from them. Those that were lucky were gunned down by our snipers were perched on the roof of the building. I was fixated on a burning body pulling itself from under the 4x4. I pulled the rifle's bolt-action as the soldier rolled over onto his back. He didn't flail about like the others; he just laid silently, his stare burnt deep into mine. It would have been kinder to put him out of his misery, but really it was to end the torture of me having to stand and watch this. I wanted to walk away, but I couldn't move.

The memory of a small burning body falling out of the school played in my mind. This wasn't the same though; those kids were innocent, these guys

Volunteer

deserved it. Didn't they? Sounds of cheering and celebration snapped me out of my thoughts.

"We did it!" Tim screamed, jumping around. I felt his enthusiasm and shook my fist in victory with a smile on my face. We did it. But I didn't see the need to celebrate this. I watched the burning carnage and bodies behind the dancing celebrations of the locals.

Then one of the guys on the roof screamed, pointing to the other side of the compound. Everyone with a gun ran to the second barricade.

"Oh Fuck!" Tim cursed as he dropped his rifle and raced towards the building where we slept. I followed, finally seeing Michael.

"Michael! What's going on?" I ran at him, desperate for someone to tell me what was going on.

"We need to go now," he yelled. "We didn't get them all." He was trying to pull me back down to our MAA 4x4.

"What? What are you talking about? We got their weapons and stuff. Their 4x4s. They've got nothing."

"We hit that patrol, but there is another coming. A larger one. We have to leave now. It's over. Let the army fight this one." He stopped to catch his breath.

"We need to get the kids and the staff out of here," I reminded him. That's why all this was happening in the first place. Just then a communal explosion of gunfire and RPGs erupted at the second barricade.

"We have no time. They'll have to make it on their own," Michael said, running backwards.

"No way! You know they'll only make it half way across the bridge, if they're lucky. Help Jenna and Tim and I'll meet you down there."

I raced to our new frontline. After the night before, I needed to see this with my own eyes. I ran along the barricade keeping low, dropping to my knees at the sound of gunfire whistling through the air. I picked a well-covered spot behind one of the old vehicles. It was badly rusted, but in the areas not exposed by the metal cancer it was a baby blue colour. Abandoned here since the fifties, like the blue car from the old Milky Way advert. I sang the tune in my head.

Volunteer

Through the broken windows an advancing LF force could be seen, and indeed, it was a sizeable patrol. Six 4x4s and a load of rebels, but two 4x4s were already in flames. So, maybe we were holding them. I took aim and fired, encouraged by the young soldier beside me. He was born for this, He looked like a soldier should: brave, focused, moulded into the uniformed image. I doubt I was hitting anything and didn't really care if I did or didn't. I was an extra gun going off. As far as I was concerned, it was all helping to halt their advance. I fired towards the ducking, diving, sprinting rebels as their bullets zipped all around us. We had them in the open and had stalled their advance, surely. I flinched at the sensation of blood spray. The soldier beside me slumped, face first, onto the ground, the arc-shaped blood stain on the car showing his descent to his death.

My body jumped and threw itself backwards at the sound of a deafening explosion as the corner of the building opposite collapsed, followed by a second blast as one of the stolen 4x4s fractured and burst into flames. A body rolled off the back and collapsed in a burning heap, rolling about on the ground. Fuck this. I had done enough. I pulled myself to my feet, flinging the rifle away carelessly, and raced back down through the compound. All our 4x4s were gone. Had they left without me?

There was another explosion and I threw myself to the wall of a building on my right. I huddled close to the ground, pulling my knees into my chest. If I lay here and played dead maybe they wouldn't notice. I was in deep shit.

"Chris! Chris!" Michael waved at me from the opposite building. I crawled on all fours, keeping low before rising to my feet to follow Michael, sprinting towards the bridge. I slid behind one of the smouldering 4x4s and I watched people run through the barricade and passed the carnage of the pile up, then across the bridge. Why weren't we doing the same?

"Where is everyone? Jenna and Tim?" My lungs burned.

"They headed on. Took as many as they could. I tried to make sure everyone headed towards the bridge, and then came back for you."

We couldn't move, exhausted in the heat. Gunfire followed us as our failing force made its way down the street. Bodies lay motionless dotted the road close to the barricade.

Volunteer

"We're fucked! We are so fucked. What did we do?" Michael shut down, hugging his knees, he shook his head. We should have just crossed the bridge when we had the chance. This was it, I guess. I stretched my legs out in front of me, my head fell back against the 4x4. Not exactly the hero's death I dreamed of. I tried to judge how close they were getting. And then, there she was.

Ila was sitting across the street, against the wall, crying and hugging her teddy.

"What the fuck is Ila doing here?" Now I had a reason not to give up. I screamed out to her. Ila's teary eyes searched the compound and once she fixed them on me she just cried harder, reaching out her hand as she had always done.

"I'm coming sweetheart. Just stay there. Fuck!" I tried to get my nerves in check. My adrenaline peaked again as bullets fizzed through the air around us. Impatient, Ila stood up and walked towards me, stopping and clenching up in fear at the sound of an explosion or gunshot, still with her small hand holding out for mine.

"No Ila! Stay there! I'm coming sweetheart! Stay there!" She didn't understand. I had no choice, I ran towards her, with Michael trying to grab me back as bullets hit the ground around us. I crouched low as I ran, not sure whether I should grab her and continue to run for cover, or sprint back to Michael. I wasn't really thinking at all.

As I reached for her hand, her body shifted away from me. My arms moved with her, but as I realised why she had moved out of my reach, my legs buckled. I slid to my knees and fell on to my side. My body shook as I screamed through gritted teeth, reaching for her little foot where she lay motionless on the ground. My breath exploded out of my mouth and I heaved. I patted her stomach with my other hand as the tears rolled down my face.

"No, no," I moaned. A thin trail of blood from the bullet wound above her left eye rolled down her face. A red tear joining the increasing puddle leaking from the back of her head. Michael was back in his defeatist huddle, hands on his head.

"Michael! I don't know what to do!" I screamed. But he didn't flinch. "Help me. Help me Michael!"

I didn't know how to fix her, I wasn't trained for this sort of injury. What was I to do? My mind raced through memories of movies, books, all of the first aid courses I had done, anything to help me. The more hopeless it appeared, the more emotional I was. I slowly pulled my T-shirt off and lifted her head, without acknowledging the spaghetti-like mess entangled around my fingers. I wrapped her head like Odette's headscarf and picked Ila up in my arms, and held her as I knelt out in the open.

"Shush. Shush. It's OK. It's OK," I whispered as I rocked her.

She was obviously dead, and I can't explain why I did that. It was the right thing at the time. I didn't know what else to do. I don't know if I was crying for her, I mean, I had only known the wee thing for a day and a half, but the tears rolled down my cheeks and dripped off my chin. Was it just by because of the sheer nature of what had happened? This was another fuck-up on my behalf; a half-hearted rescue attempt that, once again had ended in disaster. I should never have called out to her. I should have just gone and got her instead of being a fucking coward. She shouldn't have been there. I should be dead, not her.

I continued to hold her until my body stopped shaking. I knelt there motionless. Looking at nothing, thinking of nothing. If this was it, then fuck it. Nothing mattered any more. As far as I was concerned, they'd be doing me a favour. I wasn't going to fight, scream, or beg. I searched for my fate. Who would take the shot? Instead, I watched as the rebels turned in retreat. One rebel fell to the ground, and people ran from behind me and advanced up the street. The Ethiopian army had finally decided to show. Freed from his frozen state, Michael raced over to me, and pulled me up under the armpits.

"We have to go now. She's gone. You need to put her down." I nodded, but I couldn't let her go. I couldn't leave her here. Michael hauled me to my feet, desperate to leave.

"I want to go home," I muttered, emotionless.

"We're going home," Michael said.

"No, *home* home. *My* home. I can't do this anymore. I want to see my parents."

"It's OK," Michael said, helping me up.

We walked towards the bridge and I held on tight to Ila, fearing someone would take her from me. I walked blindly through the crowd, with Michael steering me by my shoulders, I was pushed and pulled through the chaos. Once we reached our

4x4, I was trailed on, refusing to free up my hands in fear of dropping my precious bundle.

We drove off and I sat with her in my arms, resting her on my lap, as she had in life. Behind us the sounds of gunfire and explosions increased, urged on by panicked screams. I looked at nothing, thought of nothing. I had nothing to say and there was nothing worth listening to. The heaviness in my chest was the only feeling I had. I thought I might pass out, or throw up, or burst into tears. But I didn't. I just sat there.

My awareness returned with the chill wind that brushed over my bare skin and formed goose bumps. I looked down to remind myself where my T-shirt was and Ila's body was gone. Only patches of blood on my trousers and forearm remained of her.

How long had I been sitting like this? I was embarrassed by my lack of awareness to my surroundings and feared I had been talking to myself. I later found out that we had stopped and Michael had gently lifted Ila from my arms. There was no reaction or sign of awareness from me and he left her at the side of the road, with my T-shirt wrapped around her head. My parting gift.

Gary McElkerney

It wasn't the right thing to do, but it was easier than explaining to the police or the Federals why a topless white man was nursing a dead black child with a T-shirt wrapped around her head. That's what he wanted to believe, at any rate. I liked like to think they would have understood, but I knew why we left her there. It wasn't right, but it didn't matter anyway.

Once we got to our truck, I applied that attitude for the rest of the journey to the clinic. I had got used to putting things to the back of my mind. What happened out in the field would stay at the back of my mind, until the next disaster.

Chapter 26: Stopped Dead

No rest for the wicked. Physically, I was dehydrated. Mentally, I needed something stronger. The events of the last few days were not discussed at the clinic, although I had a fair idea they had heard from other sources. Best we got straight back into work to keep our minds busy.

We found ourselves running, nonstop around a small town that was right on the border. I guessed - with my limited geographical knowledge of Ethiopia – that this time we were over the border, as we had never been this close to the sea before. There was a river running through the town. It wasn't a fast flowing river, more like a quarry with a trickle of water only a few metres wide. It snaked its way through silently, to the sea. Ironic that this was known as a 'fishing village.'

If I was captured, I would be up this excuse for a river without a paddle, with my passport being back in Dessie. But I was assured I would be safe enough. The rebels had bombarded the town all morning in response to a backlash from the Ethiopians a few days earlier.

There had been no warning and the consequences were devastating, they had hit so hard that smoke had blanketed the town and blocked out the sun. It still hung there. We were overwhelmed, running back and forward with stretchers, so much so that the MAA 4x4s left with their suspension straining, with the casualties at the pick-up point multiplying.

More bodies were appearing than we were bringing back. It was like an assembly point for the entire village after a fire alarm. We were open for attack, helpless; we had no armoured convoy and no military presence apart from a border patrol - and what was left of them were pulling back, what was left of them. Our only saving grace was that the rebels stayed on the other side of the river, with no real intentions of coming across.

After numerous runs, our MAA 4x4s turned up with a bus similar to the one the team had travelled about in. People were still arriving; thirty people lay around injured with their entire families

Volunteer

surrounding them, crying or in shock. Michael was standing disheartened and overwhelmed.

"You OK man?" I shouted.

"Yeah, yeah fine. We've got nothing left. All our supplies are used up. We need to get these people out of here, as quick as possible. I'll be back soon."

"Where are you going?" This was not the time to go walkabout.

"Just to have a quick look round, see what I can get." As he marched off, I screamed at the volunteers to get people on the bus, while I tried to prioritize the injured. Women and children first, then the men who needed critical care.

This was Michael's job, but we couldn't wait for him. I wish I had, it was harder than I thought. Not from a moral perspective, it was just hard to work out the extent of people's injuries. Where the fuck was Michael?

I needed him to explain to the rest of the able-bodied people that they were on their own. It was heartless to leave them here, but at the end of the day, we were here to offer medical assistance to those who needed it most. I was sick of being used as a human shield.

I ran around and helped people to their feet. Along the street, a figure emerged from the smoke and I focused on it to try and identify it as military, civilian, or worse - a rebel. Who the fuck was it? A young man and judging by his clothes a civilian. Mid-teens, maybe older. I couldn't exactly tell as he staggered up the street, the weight of his head pulled him forward and his feet followed. He had been bleeding from a head wound; the blood stained the right collar and shoulder of his grey T-shirt - that wasn't going to be easy to wash out. He was dazed, confused by his injury and the smoke. He swiped a lazy arm to clear a path. Strange, because the smoke didn't appear to be that thick. A shot rang out that caused me to jump. I watched him stumble and roll onto his back, as fearful screams came from the crowd.

I ran back close to the crowd and took off my bag, throwing it beside a family who were huddled in fear around a stretcher. I looked down the street, trying to formulate a plan.

"Don't do it!" Michael shouted, but from where? Did he have a better look? Was he closer? "Just go! Leave him."

Volunteer

"No, he's still moving. I can get him!" I shouted, as I walked to the wall.

"Just go! We have enough to deal with. You won't make it. The rebels are bound to move and in a few minutes we're going to be in range," Michael pleaded. Where was he? We could get this kid, I knew it.

"I've got this," I answered, shaking my hand dismissively.

"There is not enough cover, that sniper will pick you off. Chris, fucking leave it! We don't even have supplies." A few more shots rang out, spitting dust into the air as the bullets struck close to the kid. It only fed my reasoning. Fuck it. I pushed off the wall.

After all I had been told about hugging the walls for safety, I charged down the middle of the street. My arms and legs pumped, my heart and lungs raced. I wasn't going to change the world, or even this country, but I could make a difference for this kid, for me. I darted round large obstacles and jumped, enthusiastically, over smaller ones. As I got closer, I lowered my body to the ground, but my speed never changed.

Somewhere in the back of my mind, beyond my rationalising this action, I heard the air whistling just as the smoke lifted and revealed the hidden sky. My ears popped and a faint blanket of dust wisped across my face. The ground dropped away from me like missing a step. I was weightless, the silence ringing in my ears, as I was blown through the air. My arms instinctively covered my head and the blue sky melted into darkness.

I was completely at peace, my heart beat steadily through my weightless body. I was relaxed, a faint noise around me tried to outdo the ringing in my ears. I'd heard once that the ringing in the ears was the death of that frequency. Not sure if that was true, but it entered my mind. Suddenly, my arm moved, appearing strangely heavier than the rest of my body. It was being moved beyond my control. My body was rolled over. This was strange because I was convinced I had been lying on my back. A sudden jolt to my body, and a scraping sensation along my back.

What the hell was going on?

I couldn't open my eyes, or maybe I didn't want to. I had enjoyed the peace and quiet. But, the scraping continued randomly until it was replaced by pressure on my body. There was a voice; by its tone it seemed to be shouting, but it didn't come across as harsh.

"You stupid motherfucker!"

The words echoed around my head, in harmony with the ringing in my ears. I opened my eyes, not certain if someone had spoken the words or if it was my subconscious berating me. I tried to focus on the unfolding drama and registered other sensations: liquid flowed from my ears, like after a trip to the swimming pool. And my nose was bleeding, a familiar feeling from days fighting school bullies.

I heard a voice shout and the pressure lifted from my back. I was no longer relaxed. My body was heavy, my breathing laboured, and my skin stung as I was lifted, with my head hanging back. I tried to look around, but the pressure in my head increased and I slipped back into the comfort of darkness.

Eventually, I was lucid, and despite the convincing trickery of my mind, I worked out I wasn't on a beach after all, I understood that I was very much still in Ethiopia and I was being rushed back to the clinic.

The sound of waves was not the sound of the sea, and was in fact the engine of the MAA 4x4 that was throwing me from side to side. I asked the figure who loomed over me what had happened, but if it was Michael he was ignored me. I had a fair idea that half way down the street, a few mortar shells landed, exploding just as I passed them. Turns out they landed close enough to take me off my feet and send me crashing through a house.

Luckily for me, it was a flimsy shanty house, made of scavenged materials. Enough to cause harm if you got thrown into it, it would appear, but nothing worse. If the explosion had hit me a little further up the street, I would have been thrown into one of the more solid buildings and become a bloody mural on the front of it. The explosion had caused a smoke screen for the team, and given them enough time to get everyone on board the 4x4 and out safely. It also gave them enough time to get down to me.

Michael and the others must have been convinced I was dead, but just as I hadn't given up on the injured kid, the guys didn't give up on me. They trailed my sorry, lifeless body up the street – and hopefully that kid, too. Worth it, or so I tried to convince myself as the pain spread through my entire body.

Volunteer

Without Michael saying a word, I knew I was done. I couldn't see his face, but I knew there would be no more compassion or sympathy coming from it. This hurt, after everything we had been through. I tried to sit up, using my forearms to push me up, and fuck did that hurt.

"I'm fine. Just strap me up, I'll be grand tomorrow," I muttered. "I'll even take a day off and rest if you want. I can still do this." I wasn't ready to call it quits and I wasn't one to play the patient. But, arguing right now was not helping my case. I tried to get up and to speak but it knocked me for six, and I was close to passing out again. I knew this wasn't about my ability to do the job.

Emmanuel had warned me that if I had another close call, then that was it. The charity couldn't have my death on their hands, and this was more than a close call.

Chapter 27: No time for Goodbyes

We pulled into the clinic courtyard and I was helped to sit up in the back of the 4x4. By now I was spaced out and not taking much in. I slumped forward, my legs stretched out in front of me, muscles straining under the weight of my upper body. With a little help from anxious volunteers, I trailed myself to the edge of the truck. But, instead of helping me off, I was instructed to stay put as the equipment was lifted from around me.

The volunteers patted my shoulder as they jumped off the 4x4. Their absence lessened the strain on the suspension. Mentally, I wished them well, and waved them goodbye in my head. Physically, I was unable to move. My head dropped on to my chest and hung like a lead weight as I stared at the blurred ground. My eyes focused for a second before losing it again, like looking through a camera lens with someone messing around with the zoom.

Volunteer

Unable to lift my head, I fought to keep my eyelids to keep them open. It reminded me of the early hours of a fading house party, struggling after hours of drinking to stay awake and be part of the conversation. Every movement was an effort. I slumped forward. Hands placed either side of my head caught me as I passed the balance threshold, and started to fall. My head came to rest on something soft. I closed my eyes, craving sleep. But it was interrupted.

As my head was pushed back, my eyes opened like those on a toy doll. Odette forced a smile through her tears. She bent down and picked up a basin of water and placed it beside me. How bad did I look? Had I lost an ear or part of my head? Pretty sure that wouldn't go down well with my folks.

"You should see the other guy." I slurred, trying to lighten the situation. This raised a smile and laugh from her; laughing at me, and not with me. "Think there was, like, ten of them. They'll need more than that next time."

Odette shushed me as she got on with job in hand. I fell back into my silent, drunken state, embarrassed by my vulnerability and other people getting emotional always made me feel uneasy. I knew I should comfort them, but I never could.

Instead, I would appear cold or make a joke. I couldn't cope with crying in front of people either, and would wait until I was alone. I lacked certain emotional responses at times. She carefully dabbed at my face with a cloth. I was powerless to do anything so I closed my eyes, wanting to sleep. Wincing and shuddering now and again if the cloth ran over a graze or deep cut. The pain kept me just this side of conscious as she ran the cloth over the top of my head, through my hair, cleaning out my ears, and round the back of my neck. Then carefully, like a mother with a newborn, she rolled the bottom of my T-shirt up past the base of my ribs and up to my armpits. Then pulling at my shirt sleeve, gently pushing my arm through the hole, letting it flop onto my lap. I was useless, unable to help myself. My brain lagged and responses were slow.

I opened my eyes. The palms of my hands in my lap were stained with crusted red and brown blood. With this much blood, I should have been in a lot more pain. I could feel a faint tingling, but I knew it was only a matter of time before pain covered my body like a rash. Was this all my blood? I enjoyed the cool water on my head, my eyes followed the cloth every time it was pulled away

Volunteer

and rinsed in the basin. I watched clouds of red dying the water each time the cloth was squeezed. The water pulled the blood from the cloth as it emerged less red than it went in, but forever stained, never to be white again.

She stopped and moved away. Arms lifted me and I slid off the back of the truck. They moved me awkwardly, feet trailing on the ground; I tried to walk, but couldn't coordinate my feet for the short distance to the open door of a 4x4, where my bag waited. I was swung into the seat, my legs lifted in. I was about to seek some sort of answers to all of this. My brain finally kicked in as I opened my mouth, but I was muzzled by my own T-shirt being pulled over my head. I saw Emmanuel through my half-closed eyes lean across me and fix my seat belt. He placed some wrapping in my lap and a hand on my forehead to push it back and he placed two white tablets for me to eat in my mouth.

"This will help with the pain. I'm sorry, but you have to go. We wish it wasn't the case, but we can't risk you getting killed, especially when you've become a liability to yourself." He tipped the tablets into my mouth and lifted a bottle of water to my lips, placing his hand under my chin as he forced me to drink. I swallowed.

"Good man." He patted my chest, and left before I had a chance to speak. Odette appeared, and with one hand holding the opposite side of my face from her, she kissed my cheek, catching the edge of my lips as if she'd gone in for a real kiss, but changed her mind. A thank you whispered between my lips just as she closed the door. I heard the muffled sound of Emmanuel outside issue instructions in Amharic. The conversation faded as I was blacking out. Someone entered the driver's seat and my eyes flickered, I searched through the window my head was rested on. Odette was crying, one hand to her mouth and the other pressed against the glass. I tried to muster enough strength to match my hand with hers, that special touch, but it was physically impossible. My fingers touched the glass only for a second, then my hand flopped to my side and I drifted off.

I was woken by one of the volunteers who lifted my bag and swung it onto his shoulder before helping me out of the 4x4. The rain poured down, fat raindrops, the type that gives off a smell. The splashes on my skin were welcomed. My body was on fire and rain-soaked my T-shirt, giving me the small mercy of cooling. I wanted to stop and stand with eyes closed, head tilted to the sky. The rain was evidence that I was still alive.

Volunteer

The volunteer was in control of my body. He steered me as carefully and patiently as the waiting bus would allow. He helped me, holding my bag as we climbed on board. I concentrated on walking, not wanting to look at the people who recoiled from me. Half way up the aisle, I was deposited on an empty double seat and my bag put on my lap. The bus was packed, but the passengers kept a safe distance from me, I ignored their stares and peered out the window at the rain, surprised by its appearance in this country.

"They say when it rains here something good has happened," the volunteer said, as if he had read my mind.

I looked for Michael. Where was he? I expected him to at least see me off. I could have sworn he had helped me into the 4x4. The volunteer smiled politely, patted my shoulder, and left the bus. I couldn't speak, but hoped my face expressed the gratitude I had for his help. Where was Michael? I watched as the volunteer spoke to the driver and jumped off the bus. A figure walked to the 4x4, blurred by the water flowing down the window, he waved a hand above his head without looking back. As cool as ever. I knew he would come, after everything we'd been through. But he hadn't bothered to help me to the bus.

I rested my head on the window and watched the droplets race each other down the glass before closing my eyes. I listened to the sound of the rain beating off the roof. At the age of seven I had been packed up and moved into the attic, sold on the idea of having my own room with a new addition to the family. At first, the rain and the wind terrified me, my imagination conjured up nightmare scenarios. But it was okay because I had my blanket; blankets had been defending kids from the boogie man, ghosts and under-the-bed demons for centuries.

Now, the rhythm of the rain harmonized with my thoughts. I slumped in my seat, semiconscious, and thought of the 'could haves', 'should haves' and 'would haves' of my failed plans. Seriously, who would want to plan something like I had just been through? Sure, jump into a mortar attack, mental disintegration of my sanity for a little fun. Might be interesting?

I woke up with a start. That weird, falling sensation you get when you're asleep. The bus bumped around, signalling we were still moving, but I didn't know for how long. Nothing was familiar. I forced my head off the window, leaving a hair patterned blood print on the glass and noticed a small child was staring at me, his mother pulled at his clothes to turn him around.

Volunteer

I tried to stretch without moving my body, tightening all the muscles and trying not to make a noise. I yawned through my teeth and I took a quick look around the packed bus. The two seats in front of me, the one beside me, and the two behind me were empty. Understandable. In what country would you sit down beside a guy covered in dry blood and open wounds? I didn't care, I was going home.

Fuck, I was going home.

This might be a bad thing. How would I explain this? I had gone from being a regular guy with plenty of friends, a good social life, ambition, hobbies and a normal family - to this. I was empty, a shell of what I was before.

I was a Christian, but I couldn't turn to God because he wasn't here. He had forgotten about this place, and everyone in it, a long time ago. It was evident that he favoured the rich. God was a fictitious character, designed by mankind as someone to turn to when you couldn't speak to anyone else. It's often easier to talk to a stranger, even better if he was invisible, but my calls for help had been deleted from his voicemail messages without the decency of a returned call. My faith hadn't just been tested, it had been eradicated.

Gary McElkerney

Okay, so, I only called on the big man when I wanted something - the popular girl, success in sport or exams, rarely offering prayers of thanks and just rhyming off routine prayers in mass. I wasn't a model Christian, but who was? My prayers begging for help had been left unanswered and I would not be sold on the argument that at least I was alive, that God had looked out for me. Bollocks. Look at the state of me. Physically, I was alive. But at what mental cost? Saved my arse!

My life before wasn't perfect, but it worked, it made sense. Who would I turn to? Who would believe me? I envisioned the disappointment on people's faces at my stupidity. How would I deal with the disappointment of my parents? Their trial child shielded from the bullshit troubles of Northern Ireland, they had done a great job raising me, I was a university student, charitable and well-mannered.

My mates would think I was talking shit, trying to glorify a boring Christian charity story. It would sound like an attempt to outdo everyone else's summer; the guy that left a few weeks ago would never have lifted a gun, wouldn't have dealt with the shit I had seen. Look at me now. Pathetic, covered in my own blood, lucky that I hadn't lost a limb or end up with disfiguring scars.

Volunteer

Was this a curse for being Northern Irish? For years I had detested the narrow-mindedness of the bigots, the mindless violence that was increasingly just for 'fun', something to do around the local flash point, the cause long forgotten. I felt like crying, but I had nothing; I was empty, a shell of what I was before, a psychological wreck who couldn't think straight. So, one Northern Irish guy turns his back on the infamous 'Troubles', but ends up hunted down by worse. We had tried to walk away from the fight, and signed up to be something more than the shit that happens back home. Or maybe I was just talking shit.

I closed my eyes again and rested my head on the shuddering window. I decided it was best to say nothing and just blank it out, as though it had never happened. No one would be able to understand because they weren't there. I hoped that the person I was before was waiting to take back over when I got to Dessie. Amnesia might be my best protection. Leave unexplainable cuts and scrapes missing in time. It had to be like this, it was the only way to save what was left of me.

Chapter 28: Rewritten

I woke up in my hotel room in Dessie, and tried to focus on the blurred outlines of the room. Roisin was sitting on Paul's bed, opposite me. I hadn't even bothered to get into the bed, and had slept with my head at the bottom, legs over the side. I fixed my glasses on to my face and noticed the empty whiskey bottle on the floor. I had used the alcohol to clean my cuts when I finally got back last night, using the wraps Emmanuel had given me, and then drank the rest to help me sleep.

I forced myself up, shifting the weight from my injured forearm to my hand, wincing. I lifted my eyes to meet Roisin's and waited for the barrage of abuse. I was tired, or maybe still drunk. There it was; pain coursed through my body like boiling water and there was a duller pain in my stomach and chest. I was nauseous, either from the wounds, or the drink, or from sitting up too quickly. Whatever

Volunteer

the cause, I was going to throw up. I swallowed, and tried to clear my mind.

"Thank God you're back and not too badly injured. Dr. Ferrere rang to tell us you were in a car accident and on your way. You look awful. Are you in much pain?" I was confused. A car accident?

"Yeah. I...I'm fine, just shaken up. First time in a car accident," I said, trying to convince myself.

"Well, we expected the worst. We are so relieved to have you back in one piece. The doctor said you were in a bad way, but that you looked worse. I saw the bandages in the bin. There was a lot of blood around the place."

We sat in an awkward pause. I guess I was supposed to say something here, but wasn't sure what. "You certainly gave us a fright," Roisin continued, to fill the gap. "You do look better than what we expected."

How bad were they thinking I was going to be? Missing legs or something?

"The clinic said you were a great help and were sorry to lose you."

Gary McElkerney

I wasn't sure of how much truth was in that comment. Was I of any use, or had I been more of a hindrance? She stood up. Was that it? No abuse for deserting the team? For not being in touch? Christ, I hadn't even contacted my parents the three weeks I had been here. My mum was going to have a freak out after telling me to keep in touch due to my lack of communication on previous trips. Emmanuel had given me a life line, the foundations to build a story around. I needed to think fast and come up with a simple yet consistent story.

"We have two more days on site, then a day before we head back to Addis Ababa. If you feel up to it, the team would like to see you. You have been missed. It would be good for the whole team to finish up on site. If you're not up to it, don't worry." She smiled, with genuine relief.

I sat for a while. I didn't know whether to get up and get washed or lie down again. The door opened and Paul, mucked up to the eyeballs, came through. He'd probably been stood outside waiting for Roisin to finish.

"You're up?"

I nodded and with open palms I gestured that I was indeed up. I said nothing, a little embarrassed,

Volunteer

but also trying to sense what the overall feeling was at my return. Was it one of relief and excitement, or disappointment and resentment?

"I honestly thought you would be in a coma for days." Paul dropped his mud-caked boots at the door and threw his bag at the foot of his bed. He flopped backwards onto the mattress and rolled onto his side to face me.

"Was a shock to see you back. And man did this room stink of alcohol. You must have had one hell of a party by yourself. I tried to wake you, as did Colin and Roisin, but you were never waking up in a million years. You were completely out for the count."

Who was I talking to here? This wasn't the Paul I'd left two weeks ago. He was covered in mud, wearing black combats that had been cut off badly at the knee. His white socks were stained at the top where they'd been unprotected by his boots, his grey T-shirt was also cut up and turned into a vest and covered in mud. He still wore that stupid fisherman style hat though, a reminder of his former self.

"You have a mud fight or something?" I asked to avoid the questions that were bound to follow. I hadn't had time to work out my story yet. Somehow my first few days at the clinic would have to be expanded to last the two weeks. I would take experiences from previous trips and mould it around the clinic and the people I had met. Then there was the trip to the school. Yeah, maybe not such a good idea. The memories of the first visit fed like a relay to the day after. They were as fresh as ever.

"... so yeah, not a lot of work done, but it was a good laugh," Paul chuckled to himself. He had talked the entire time and I had missed the conversation from someone lying two metres from me.

"Sounds good," I improvised. "The team are well then?"

"We've had our ups and downs," Paul rolled onto his back. "A few arguments, tears, the usual. But overall, yeah, the team is fine, been a good week. What about you? Taking on the world by yourself? You're mad man. No offence, but you look like shit. Must have been some crash."

There was a knock on the door and in walked Claire, Nicola, and Cat D. Saving grace.

"Holy shit, Chris! State of you! You just can't be normal like the rest of us," Claire

Volunteer

exclaimed. And like a good cop–bad cop routine, Nicola jumped in.

"How are you feeling? What was it like?" Nicola was definitely my type. Blonde and naturally beautiful, she had curves in all the right places. The type of girl who was attractive, but didn't think of herself that way, with bright blue eyes that could buy and sell me. She was a genuine girl with a great personality and good for a laugh. The type you could playfully take the piss out of and she would see the funny side and give as good as she got.

"What was the crash like?" I asked, puzzled.

"No! Your trip away. How was that?" She rolled her eyes, smiling as she shook her head.

"Trip was OK, nothing too exciting, really," I said, "The crash certainly got the heart rate going, but wouldn't recommend it." I was thankful to avoid details.

I spent the last two days on site and despite momentary freezes as I let sharp pains subside, I put in the effort of the missed two weeks. The attitude of the group hadn't changed that much. In fact, less work was done each day. But who was I to comment? No one asked for details of my trip, but they did ask after my health with concern and I covered the majority of my injuries with a long sleeve T-shirt. I volunteered to break rocks at the bottom of the dried up lake, smashing them without taking a break, and never gave anyone the chance to help. I must have looked deranged as I put all my anger and frustration to good use, ignoring the pain. I tore my hands apart, abusing muscles that were already battered, using the sledge-hammer as an outlet for it all.

At the start there was a group of about fifteen people waiting for their turn, but by the end of the day there was one old man left, who sat with a small group of rocks he held with his feet and smashed up with a small hammer. He tapped them and they split with little effort. Occasionally, he stopped to watch my brute strength, which did nothing but make for more work and effort.

After watching my psychotic rock smashing episode, Paul decided to be the one to ask me about my trip during dinner. Everyone quietened down to listen. I began nervously, telling the group about the clinic, basing my story on the first few days there. I told them of trips to local schools and playing football. Visiting orphanages and hiking trips to remote villages. The group was captivated, almost jealous of what I'd seen and experienced. Their questions gave me the opportunity to refine the story. I praised all the work done by Medical Aid Africa and by each volunteer, whose sacrifice and dedication was something to admire. This was the truth. I was careful not to boast or give myself praise. I wanted to avoid unnecessary questions.

They were sold, as was I.

Chapter 29: Increased Suspicions

With a few days left before we headed home, we drove north to the city of Lalibela. I, like everyone, connected this with the Hotel Lalibela, but we had never known the significance.

As the story goes, there once was a king, Lalibela, who had a vision that he was commissioned by God to construct thirteen churches in eleven years. Instead of building the churches, he had them carved out of the ground and we had the privilege of seeing these wondrous creations.

For the first time, I witnessed something normal by tourist standards. Something that was of real value to this country, giving it its own identity. Something that no other country had. The detailing was primitive in comparison to intricate European sculptures, nevertheless you couldn't ignore the fact that this was carved out of one piece of earth. I wasn't looking at a shed or a mud hut, I was looking

Volunteer

at something out of an adventure movie: two to three-storey structures the size of small warehouses carved with doors, windows, statues, ornate with decoration inside and out, even guttering. Some had scaffolding around them with a corrugated roof to protect them from acid rain. We didn't see all the temples, but did visit the signature church that I recognised from postcards; the church of Saint George.

We stood out the front of the church and sat around the shaded, carved walls, resting and hidden from the sun. We had been on the go from nine that morning, continuously travelling on foot or by mule through the midday heat. This was the only time we had the chance to rest. Some of the team took advantage of the shade, with the attitude that if you had seen one, you had seen them all.

Strictly, that wasn't true. Yes, the concept was the same. But the design and most of the decoration was unique.

Negasi had been inside the church as he had every church. Curiosity got the better of me and I climbed the age worn steps, with the wonder of an explorer discovering the temple for the first time. After watching my exaggerated approach Negasi spoke, "You like to look inside?" Startled I looked around to see if anyone else was watching.

"Am I allowed to?" I asked.

"Why would you not?" Negasi gestured for me to enter.

"Because I'm not Muslim?"

"Nonsense." And with that, Negasi led me inside.

It was cool and dark. Light from tiny windows illuminated vibrant coloured rugs on the floor, carved figures embedded in the walls, and an altar with what I suspected was the Muslim equivalent of a cross. It was quiet and peaceful, and I wanted to stay. Outside there was the carnage, in here I was safe. Safe from judgement. A stranger with no past. All the while, I could feel Negasi's eyes focused on me.

"Peaceful?" Negassi asked.

"Yeah, you wouldn't think it with that lot outside. The carvings are incredible."

It was one of those wonders that you wouldn't find anywhere else. And here I was in this time, in this moment, a moment that would remain in my life and no one else's. Negasi smiled.

"Are you peaceful?"

"Yeah," I said. "It has that effect on me. I feel at ease. Nice and cool in here." I knew what he was asking, but I tried to bluff my way out of it with silence.

"You may hold visible scars of conflict on your skin, but I can see in you the horrors of my country. The invisible scars on the inside."

My heart stopped and a chill moved over my body. How the fuck did he know? With a soft pat on my shoulder he left to re-join the group, leaving me there in the shrouded silence of the church, motionless like the carved statues on the wall hiding their own secrets.

On the way back to the hotel we stopped at a shop where Colin and Roisin were picking up supplies for the leaving party that night. I exited the bus too, with no real intention of helping, but at hand if they needed me. I stood for a second on the last step of the bus and lifted a bottle to my mouth, draining the last mouthful of warm water. A small boy ran towards me, a cheeky grin on his face, and I knew full well what he was after.

Gary McElkerney

He held out his hand and asked for the bottle in Amharic. I had found it a hard language to learn and my understanding hadn't improved much. I hadn't had to fend for myself with Michael as my translator. Regardless of whether I spoke the language or not, I knew how this encounter played out. The children from the building site would do a quick clean-up of all the plastic bottles at the end of the working day. Once he had the bottle, out would come the begging hand, the puppy eyes, expectant flat palm.

The rule was simple: you didn't give money or food unless you had enough to give all the children. Not that there were lots of them, but we had heard of them being bullied and beaten for money. This time, I didn't have any money on me. So, shaking my head, I emptied out my pockets to visually demonstrate my lack of coinage. I stepped off the bus and sat on the bottom step. I laughed at his persistence, his patient hand, convinced I had something to give him. I shrugged and shook my head.

"I've no money," I repeated, knowing he understood even if he couldn't speak English. I flinched at a movement to my right. The boy dropped to floor. Squeals of outrage poured from the bus and I tried to grab the kid before he hit the ground, a stream of blood ran from above his left eye mixing with his tears and he cried out.

A Federal had hit the child with the butt of his rifle and was now kicking him along like a tin can. This was my fault, I had relaxed too much in the company of the team and I had let my guard down, slipped into my old ways. Everything went quiet and slowed down, I fixed my eyes on him, a red mist smothered my senses and my jaw clenched as if I might break my own teeth. My stomach sank and I shook violently from the adrenaline rush. I launched myself at the Federal, and grabbed for his rifle, pulling at it with both hands, I threw my shoulder into him and caught him off-balance mid kick. He let go of the rifle as he tried to save himself from hitting the ground, his hands reached out to grab at the air. No sooner had he imprinted a shape in the dirt than he was back on his feet, aggressively upright.

"What?" I screamed as I squinted down the barrel of the rifle I now aimed at his head. "What you going to do now?"

The calls from the bus had turned into terrified screams as I remained locked on the Federal. He was younger than me and he matched my gaze, his body language showed no fear, but his eyes watered. There was a commotion either side of me as the others got up to speed with situation. On one side I heard the panicked voices of Negasi, Amare, Colin and Roisin trying to figure out what was going on. Shocked to see me with a rifle in my hand. On the other side, a noise clicked in my head, and it reminded me of my inability to think before I acted; it was the sound of a bolt-action.

Had I assessed the situation, I would have remembered that the Federals patrol in groups of four. On hearing the bolt-action, a sensible person would have dropped the gun and surrendered. But not me, I was making a point and was too stubborn. I wasn't backing down. I had done too much of that already. My logic was simple. I pull the trigger, blow this Federal's head off. As the bullet left the barrel I would be on the ground, holier than a sieve, blown away by his counterparts. I heard Negasi pleading in Amharic to the Federals behind me while Amare implored in my ear. Colin and Roisin torn between comforting those on the bus and screaming at me. I was finding it hard to focus on everything that was happening as I tried to figure out my next move.

"You need to put the gun down Chris, before this gets out of hand," Amare warned. Was he kidding me? This was already out of hand. It was hard to imagine how anyone was walking away from this, and I didn't care if I never did. "It's OK. Just give him back the gun and we can go. No one needs to get hurt, above all you." Amare edged closer, his hands reaching out. He was not taking this gun off me. The Amharic voices escalated from discussion to argument.

"Please, I pray you." Negasi said his soft hand landed on my back.

I removed my left hand from the rifle and slowly raised my hands in a gesture of surrender, the AK47 pointing into the air. The voices hushed into a low hue of suspense.

It was Negasi's simple touch that reached me. Yes, I was quite happy to die. But once my gun went off they were all going to shoot, with Amare, Negasi, Colin, and Roisin in the firing line.

One of the Federals took hold of the gun and lifted the weight off me. As the rifle slipped past my fingers, the Federal I'd held hostage burst into a rant and stepped aggressively forward. Rather than admit I was in the wrong or offer an apology, I went straight for him. Again, in a stand-off, this time unarmed, with Negasi, Amare, and Colin pulling at my T-shirt, they tried to get me on the bus. The Federal was being held back by his colleagues.

"Come on then you fucking wanker! What the fuck you going to do? I'd rip your head off you fucking prick!" I screamed, trying to force myself between Negasi and Amare with one hand, while trying to grab at the soldier with the other. I can only imagine the same was coming from his mouth, his actions were mirroring mine. I wanted to fight the world, starting with this guy. I was fine to take them on and whatever they threw at me. Anger was bursting the seams of my body and the arms holding me back were containing it. The situation wasn't helped when one of the other young Federals, with the thinnest excuse for a moustache, pushed Negasi and set me off again. Notching my anger up a gear.

"Touch him again and I'll break your fucking arm!" I warned, as I stabbed a finger in his face. Negasi and Amare looked terrified, but not of the Federals; the Northern Irish accent is harsh at the best of times, but worse when used in anger.

"Chris, just get on the bus!" Colin screamed over the commotion. "You've made your point."

"Right, let me go! Let me go!" I shrugged off the guarded hands and walked backwards,

Volunteer

keeping my eye on the Federal before I turned and stepped onto the bus.

I was greeted by shocked silence and embarrassed eyes, not knowing where to look. Was I embarrassed? Fuck no, and why should I be? Roisin, who had made her way onto the bus to comfort a hysterical Orlaith, glared at me and shook her head in disgust. "What?" I questioned loudly and angrily.

"Nothing!"

"Should I have done nothing? Just stood there like the rest of you and pretend it wasn't happening? Watch an innocent child get kicked around? Hoping it would all end well? You know what, it wouldn't have. It never does. Open your fucking eyes."

"That's enough Chris!" Colin shouted down the bus. "Sit down!"

"You can fuck up too!" I glared back at him.

I slowly sat down among smirks, muffled comments, and whispers. I stared out the window breathing heavily through my nose trying to calm down, my jaw wired shut. I glared around the bus, challenging anyone to meet my burning gaze, there was only Mark, who gave a nod of approval.

Amare fell into his seat, exhausted by the incident and wiped his forehead with a white handkerchief. Negasi walked down the bus towards me and with every step the bus grew quieter. I fully expected another argument or even the possibility of being hit by the one man I didn't want to disappoint or offend. I avoided his fixed stare as he stopped by my seat. I looked at his sandals. He always wore the same pair of sandals. Slowly I met his gaze and braced myself for the anticipated barrage of abuse. It never came. Instead, he put out his right hand. I was confused. Slowly, I took his hand in mine, cautious that it might be a trap. But as his grip tightened his other hand tapped my shoulder and he nodded with thankful eyes, then turned back and took the driver's seat.

What the fuck was that? The engine fired and the bus jolted forward. I stared down at nothing and tried to process what had just happened. Was I out of order? Did he approve of my actions, aware that I had stood up against injustice and fought for that kid? Or was it something completely different, his way of calming me down. Maybe he understood what I was going through, even if I didn't. Was it

Volunteer

simply for making the right decision and ending the situation with my pride being the only casualty?

I hoped that would be the end of it but I should have known better. On our return to the hotel, Colin and Roisin called me into the sunroom for a 'quick chat'. I flopped down onto the seat like an obnoxious teenager, giving the impression I was still annoyed. I wasn't. I was strangely calm about the whole incident. I was pretty sure one of these two would set me off again, though.

"Interesting trip today?" Colin smirked.

I fantasized about punching him in the face.

"Is everything OK?" Roisin asked. She was concerned and that scared me a little. Why the fuck did she care all of a sudden?

"Is this about your friend, the guy you worked with?" She snapped her fingers at Colin, trying to create the spark to ignite both their brains. "Oh what's his name?"

"Michael?" Colin offered. My ears pricked up. How did they know about Michael?

"Yes, Michael. Is this about Michael?" Roisin sat forward engaged in a one to one pose with me. Colin no longer a part of the interaction.

"Is what to do with Michael?" I asked, confused, "What has he got to do with anything?"

"Doctor Ferrere told us about the death of your friend Michael, and how you weren't coping with it or hadn't fully registered the situation." Roisin was calm, unlike me.

"What are you talking about?" I asked, "Michael isn't dead." Was this a sick joke? A way of getting at me for walking out on the team? These two had a shit storm coming their way if it was! I watched their reactions, as they looked at each other with grave concern.

"He's not dead. Sure I saw him on the 4x4 on the way to clinic after ... after the crash. Fuck sake I was talking to him. He saved me."

I really needed to be careful here, I was in danger of giving myself away if they only knew the 'car crash' story. Maybe they were trying to trick me into giving myself away.

"Doctor Ferrere told us all about the crash. You were thrown from the 4x4, but unfortunately,

Volunteer

Michael was trapped," Colin said, he continued in a gentle tone, "You were badly injured, but tried to save him, there was an explosion, or a fire? He didn't make it out. Doctor Ferrere asked us to keep an eye on you, concerned you would blame yourself."

I knew it was my cue to talk, but I was confused on all fronts. Was Michael dead? Was I in a car crash? I knew I wasn't. I would have remembered something of the crash, so where did Michael fit in with my last day up north?

"Are you OK, Chris? You look a bit pale." Roisin touched my hand and I pulled away.

"Yeah I ... I'm going to get a shower before dinner. Get some water into me as well. Bit dehydrated." I threw out my excuse, and left, desperate to get back to replay the memories of what happened that day. This scenario didn't make sense.

Where was Michael?

I lay back on my bed and it clicked. I wasn't sure if my mind was playing out its own version of events, manipulated with the sudden realisation of Michael's death, or if I had recovered the missing pieces of the puzzle. The casualty walking up that street, hit by the sniper, was that Michael? No. It couldn't have been. But he had to have been close.

Even if I had known how it would end, I wouldn't have left the guy behind. Bastards must have tried to kill two birds with one stone, and they almost succeeded. Was the casualty the bait? Did they know I would try to save him? Or did they just see Michael as a local.

It still didn't make sense though. I could hear him, but I couldn't see him as my mind flicked between images of Michael crouching behind a wall to images of him being the casualty.

Surely he was the one that helped lift me out of there. Wasn't I talking to him on the 4x4 on the way to the clinic? That was him hovering over me and checking on me. I couldn't make out his face, though. Just a shape, a silhouette blocking out the sun. Was that even him? Oh fuck, tell me we didn't leave him behind. Had I left him behind?

I welled up, lifting my pillow from behind my head and pushed it over my face.

"You OK man?" Paul came out of the bathroom.

Volunteer

"I'm fine," I mumbled through the pillow, and tried to hide the quiver in my voice from holding back tears. Despite the heaviness in my chest, I wasn't going to cry in front of Paul. The worst thing was not knowing. I didn't even know his surname. Would his family have been told? Did he have a family? He had seen me at my most vulnerable, dragged me through the worst situations, and pulled me out the other side. The one time he needed me, I failed him. Above all, I had lived with this guy for the last couple of weeks and knew nothing about him.

To be fair, I had never told him much about myself either. We never really take the time to truly get to know someone. The only information we take on board is that which benefits us in some way, like the strengths and weaknesses of a person that we can use or manipulate. Using their insecurities against them, to deflect attention away from our own.

With Michael dead who could I turn to? Who else would understand my failures? Who would know how to cope with the recurring images as my mind tried to rewrite negative realities into false positives? Did we do more harm than good? Did we save more than we lost? It never felt like it. In the end, it was what it was. Nothing was going to change that, but remembering Michael as the guy who burnt up in a car crash was an insult to everything he had achieved.

He was dead. The pressure built around my nose and cheekbones. My jaw clenched. My body shook. I pressed the pillow harder around my face, fearing the anger and frustration would break free. I held it back. What difference would it make? It wouldn't change a thing.

Michael was dead.

Chapter 30: Home

I stood alone on the footpath outside the youth club. It was late evening, not quite dark, but fuck was it cold. A typical 'warm' summer's night in Northern Ireland, the only thing missing was the rain. The team members had all disappeared with their families, their safe return celebrated with joy.

I had declined lifts, telling them my dad was on his way, which wasn't true. He would be playing a gig, like every other Friday night, but I didn't need to put on a fake smile for a taxi driver and pretend the trip was everything I had hoped, which couldn't be further from the truth. I stood alone in the empty street. My mobile phone buzzed the arrival of messages sent over the last month, they could wait until tomorrow, reading them was the first step back into my old life.

Gary McElkerney

The taxi pulled up beside me and the driver beeped the horn twice. He wound down the window.

"Johnston?" He shouted in a broad accent, like I was two hundred metres away. I nodded and threw my bag into the back seat before climbing in the passenger seat.

"You away somewhere?" He asked.

"Yeah," I replied. I couldn't be assed with this rigmarole; I just wanted to get home.

"Where were you then?" He asked

"Ethiopia," I replied, hoping my short answers would deter him.

"Did you spend your time in the shade?" He laughed, "Not much of a tan going on there!"

Ah, the old Northern Irish humour. I was not in the mood for it.

"What were you doing over there then?" He persisted.

"First aid, building houses and stuff," I answered.

"Oh aye," he acknowledged, "There is a lot of people do that. One of the guys in the depot, his

Volunteer

kid was doing something like that. Don't think it was in Ethiopia though."

"So, you been on long tonight?" I asked.

Yeah, I went there, anything to get off this topic and waste some time on what was the longest five-minute journey ever.

I finally arrived home to find my mum asleep on the sofa. No welcome party or tears of joy for my return, this was home. I gently shook her.

"I'm home," I whispered. She sat up and stretched out for a hug.

"Are you hungry?" She asked. "There's some dinner in the fridge from earlier."

"I'm OK," I said, "We got a McDonald's on the way up from Dublin." We hadn't, and I was hungry, but I knew that would lead to questions. I was too tired, and I hated leftovers.

"I'm wrecked after travelling so I'm going to head to bed. Thanks."

"Okay, I'm glad you're home. Sure, you can tell us about your trip tomorrow," Mum said. "If you want to sort your washing out in the morning you can throw it in the machine first."

I nodded, kissed her cheek and headed to my room.

I sat on the edge of my bed in the attic and the rain came. Its arrival, announced by the battering on the skylight, triggered a memory. I was back, sitting on that bus, injured. I felt the blood running down the back of my head and shoulder, isolating pain to certain areas of my body. The version of me who had left a month ago never came back. As long as I had my story straight and fool-proof, with enough detail to deter questions, I knew people could be convinced.

Dealing with people I could do. Dealing with my head was harder.

I needed to switch off.

Chapter 31: Afterlife

For the next few weeks I played the part well. The more I told the story, the more convinced I became of its legitimacy. I recounted it with enthusiasm and humour, creating fictional characters that people related to. I made the limited amount of photographs I had fit the tale, but it never occurred to me to factor in a parent's ability to know their child. My mum knew something was wrong, maybe because I would brush over the 'car crash' to explain the cuts and bruises I came home with or because my story was so precisely repetitive, it sounded scripted.

Adverts promoting the good work of charities in Africa annoyed me. The soft voice of an actor, who had never stepped foot on that continent, a crying child, with swollen stomach and pleading eyes, whose life is magically transformed to full colour and bright smiles by your donations. It was as effective as 'Liking' a status on Facebook to cure cancer. Never mentioned were the losing battles.

Gary McElkerney

How about you show a dead child discarded at the side of the road, or piles of charred bodies in the street from an attack that we failed to defend because we were too busy fighting a war for oil or kicking the crap out of ourselves. Not everything was negative, there were those volunteers around the world unseen, unheard doing what they could. It just wasn't enough. So much more could be done.

The silence of the night was the most difficult. The smallest thing pulled me to the front lines again, a siren, a smell, the sound of my nephew crying, even the rain or the uncomfortable heat in the house. Staring blindly into the darkness, eyes filled with tears, I would hold back from sobbing for fear of being heard. I tried to block it out, but only ended up with graphic images playing out like a computer game. Remembering faces and mixing up my fake story with reality.

I struggled to control my mind and it pushed at my sanity until I was on the edge of my bed, knife at the base of my throat, willing my hands to drive it in deep. I wanted this to end, but. I couldn't do it. I wish I could say it was because I found some self-worth, or that my life meant more to me, or that I couldn't do it to my family and friends, or I feared that my nephew would be sent in to wake me and find a relieved corpse stuck to the blood-soaked carpet. While I had considered all of these, the fact was I was a coward. I couldn't face the pain, or the take the risk that I might get it wrong and end up disfigured with more questions to answer, which would then lead to more lies. I couldn't cope with the lies I had already told.

I had all but given up on friends and university. I no longer had a connection to anything or had any purpose in this new, artificial life. I wanted to be back in Ethiopia. There I had a purpose, I was needed, and my life meant something, not just to those I stood beside and those I helped and saved. I had self-worth, it meant something to me. Being home, I was another name, another number, an unfulfilled nobody, daydreaming through life. Instead, I racked up hours in the university design studio alone. I was a breathing corpse doing life.

I was annoyed and frustrated with the contradictions in this life. I wanted people to leave me alone, yet I needed the comfort of someone I trusted. Why couldn't they just know what I had been through without me having to explain? Why couldn't they see past this façade? I wanted to scream, let out the anger that had built up and wreck everything around me. I was angry because I thought I was stronger than this, capable of dealing with it. I was surrounded by friends and family, but I couldn't talk to any of them. I wanted to reach out, but couldn't as neurological warfare would kick off in my head.

I was alone, but it had to be that way. Everyone else's life was so perfect and settled. They fluttered about without a care in the world while I continued to smile and pretend everything was just fine.

For weeks I was unaware of the eyes of concerned friends, but Marie was there every day. Marie had always been there, from day one of my university life. A quiet, shy Dutch girl not yet corrupted by Northern Ireland, she had an open mind, which she exercised on me, introducing me to cultures, food, ideas, events, people and music I might never have noticed otherwise.

Every day she would come to the studio and invite me to lunch. I was always grateful, but always declined. She brought me coffee, then progressed to bringing her lunch and eating it in the studio with me. We talked and I became immersed in someone else's life. She never asked about the trip, but she knew something was wrong, and knew me well enough not to ask.

Volunteer

We fell into our old routine of pints between classes in the nearest pub, concerts, all night parties and crashing at each other's houses. I tried to fit the 'new' me into the old routine and I realised I owed her an explanation, but the only one I had was the truth. In an effort to cling onto our friendship, a drunken breakdown, huddled on the back step of her student digs unveiled an edited version of the truth and we developed a relationship of patience and understanding.

After months of wallowing in self-pity behind an emotional closed door, I began to notice a change. I wasn't the same person who came back emotionally shattered. I was stronger. Though I still often doubted my sanity, I began to understand that what was truly important was that I lived through the experience. I had volunteered to put myself in it, regardless of what I had expected.

Now my life was changing. I was more secure dealing with first world problems. I found I could live with my own company, in silence, without the need for technology to entertain my western boredom. My confidence grew and I was more assertive. I had the ability to strive for success. I used my ever-present pain and anger as a fuel at times, to focus, to provide that extra push that carried me over personal finish lines.

Finally, I wasn't afraid to try things outside my comfort zone and could push myself further physically, emotionally and mentally than ever before.

I had seen the best of me, but also the worst. I was all that was real and honest, an example of love and compassion, of innocence and naïvety. I was also what was dark and evil, manipulative and destructive, selfish and hateful. I had reverted to my animal instincts, not just in order to survive, but to gain the upper hand. I was humanity.

I was part of a humanitarian crisis that no one knew about. Was it better to live in ignorance of the problems of other's? I had wanted to change the world and I had failed. I didn't necessarily make it worse, but I added to everything that was wrong about it. I didn't know who I was now, but then again, I couldn't remember who I was before, and no one knows who they really are anyway.

One thing that was for certain, I was a volunteer.